The Truth Shall Make You Dead

by

Kenneth Bennight

ISBN: 978-1-946418-00-5

Table of Contents

Chapter 1: Deputy Bruhn

I didn't know the son-of-a-bitch, but I took an immediate dislike.

"Step out of the car, pal, and show me some ID." The officer rested his right hand on the butt of his Dirty Harry revolver and held a clipboard in his left. His nametag read, BRUHN. The patrol car proclaimed him a Deputy Sheriff. The Komensky County Welcome Wagon.

I stepped into a chill, wet breeze and handed over my private investigator's license and my handgun license. The pines lining the street lent their scent to the air.

Bruhn, a young, skinny man who was a good six inches shorter than I, had a pencil-neck, which made his collar too big. An oversized cowboy hat perfected the impression of a kid wearing his father's clothes. Even so, he affected a self-important swagger.

"You got a driver's license, amigo?"

"Yep."

He took that, too. Leafless trees lined the street, and a winter-brown lawn extended beyond. Intermittent raindrops plopped on my head and ran down the back of my neck. The air carried the scent of dampness and a nearby wood fire.

"Ig—NAY—zo Per—EZZ," he read off the papers.

"Close, I guess. Just call me 'Nacho.' "

"You a pri—vate DEE—tec—tive?" The man had a Napoleon complex.

"Last time I checked, that's what it said."

"You got a weapon on you, Mr. Private Detective Nacho?"

"Nope." My .45 lay in the car.

"Assume the position."

The lawyer who had hired our agency had described a corrupt system, and this clown was giving me my first taste of it—a lawman who thought his whim was unchecked.

I turned, spread my legs, leaned forward, and put my hands on my car's roof. Bruhn placed his clipboard on the roof of my car, nudged my feet back, and patted me down. When he got to my thighs, a cold gust of wind made me flinch.

"Enjoying this a bit too much, are you, Mr. Nacho?"

Cabrón. "Was I speeding, officer? I tried to hold it to twenty, even though there aren't any signs."

"Twenty, huh? Well, there's an admission. The speed limit's fifteen on this campus. I'm giving you a ticket, Mr. Private Detective Nacho." He shifted some papers on his clipboard. "Now, you just stay right where you are. Keep your hands visible at all times." He walked to the rear of my car, made notes, and then moved to the shelter and warmth of his vehicle to complete the paperwork.

Damn. Another ticket will mess up my deferred adjudication. Do these people report these tickets to the state? Drizzle soaked me as Bruhn took his time with the paperwork. He regularly looked up at me and grinned. Keeping me out in the weather must have given him jollies.

He braved the elements and handed me the ticket. "We don't get many private detectives." He started to leave, turned back, and stuck a finger in my face. "Watch yourself."

I risked prolonging the encounter. "Would you please point me to the main administration building?"

He paused. Looking me up and down as if for the first time, he pointed in the direction I had been traveling. "Big brown building ahead and to the right. Why're you headed there?" He tilted his head and raised his eyebrows.

What to tell Barney Fife? It would have prolonged the exchange to tell him my client was a lawyer suing the college. "I'm told I'm not too old to learn. Classes may be just the thing for me."

"Shit. You wouldn't be here on that bookstore business, would you? We don't need nobody stirring up trouble."

"I generally try to fix trouble, Officer, not stir it up." The S.O.B. knew exactly why I was there. Word got around in Komensky.

"You hang around here, Mr. Private Detective Nacho, and you'll get more education than you bargained for."

Bruhn walked back to his car, and I fired up my engine. My rearview mirror showed him speaking into the radio clipped to his chest. The number on his car was 13—apparently not my lucky number.

4

Chapter 2: Mark Fannin

The two-story administration building dated from the Depression. Large, square columns ran across the front. The edifice had two inscriptions above the main steps: "Komensky County Community College," and beneath that, "Ye shall know the truth, and the truth shall make you free." I wasn't betting they tried to live up to that.

I parked in a visitor's space and hustled up the steps to get out of the rain. From the top, I spotted a second cop vehicle parked at the corner of the net street. The officer was pointing binoculars at me. I waved.

Mark Fannin, the man I was looking for, had said his office was number 276. I trudged through the building, leaving a trail of drips from my soggy clothes. After wandering a maze of corridors, I found offices numbered in the 270s. The door to 276 stood open. I walked into a windowless room—little more than a closet.

A chubby, balding man with thick glasses rose and motioned to me. He wore creased slacks, a starched shirt, and a corduroy sport-coat. "Ignacio Perez?"

"Nacho, please." Soft hands. A whiff of sandalwood from his aftershave hit me.

I took in his office: light beige walls covered with Scotch-taped pictures drawn by children: butterflies, rainbows, and what seemed to be a self-portrait of a young girl with "I love you Daddy" printed awkwardly across the bottom.

"Have a seat. Looks like you've been out in the weather."

"Yeah. A local deputy kept me standing by my car." A vinyl chair let me sit without my wet clothes ruining something.

"Let me guess. Was he named Bruhn?"

"How'd you know?'

"Heh. Get a ticket?"

"For doing twenty in a fifteen. Can you believe it?"

He chortled. "Around here? You bet, but you can beat the ticket. City rules don't apply on campus, and the college administration never took any traffic-control stuff to the board of trustees. Nothing's been formally authorized." He threw his hands up. "Tickets get dismissed all the time, but enough people pay that the school still makes money."

"So they prey on the ignorant?"

A smirk covered his face. "You're surprised?"

I pointed at a photograph on his desk showing him, a woman, and two young girls. "Your family?" In the image Fannin was standing behind the seated woman, his hand on her shoulder. The younger girl was sitting in the woman's lap, and the older was leaning her head on Fannin.

He glanced at the picture, and his face warmed. "You bet. It's a couple of years old. The girls are ten and seven now."

"Cute kids."

"They change your life, but always for the better." His eyes gleamed as he looked at the picture. "You have a family?"

"A grown daughter, but she lives in Omaha, works for the railroad. My wife died a few years ago." I looked down and pushed my tongue against my lower lip. "We haven't talked much since her mother died. No falling out. It's just that, with my wife not around to initiate the calls, we both got busy." I shifted in my chair. "Partly, I'm not good with idle chitchat. You can't spend the whole time talking about the weather."

"I hear you. Mine are too young for me to worry about that. Well, how did you get to be a private detective?"

I raised both palms. "Happenstance. I retired from the Marine Corps and moved back home to San Antonio."

"Marines, huh? The drill instructors are supposed to be real bastards."

I chuckled. "Damn straight. I was one."

"Oops." He laughed.

"Anyway, I needed work and a friend suggested talking to John Michelson. He needed help for his detective agency. We hit it off." I grinned. "For one thing, we share a fondness for bourbon and cigars."

Fannin smiled. "Bourbon and cigars. A secure foundation for friendship."

I cut off the opening pleasantries. As I said, I'm not good at them. "So what's your role at the college?"

"Since telling the Texas Rangers what's going on, my only fixed duty is to keep a fresh pot of coffee going. That's also when they switched me to this new office." He gestured around the room.

"Hence the whistleblower suit and your lawyer hiring me."

"Yeah. I came here a year ago as accounting manager. I'd been unemployed for three years after being laid off by Grant Thornton. They must've figured desperation would make me overlook anything." He stopped, bit his upper lip, and shook his head. "But some things you just can't overlook." He took a deep breath. "Hell, they had set me up to be the fall guy when things unraveled. How big a fool did they take me to be?"

"Michelson told me about some bookstore shenanigans, but he didn't give me details."

"I'll show you."

He led me to the bookstore at the back of the first floor. Better lighting and brightly colored paint set the store apart from the rest of the building. Hip-hop blared from a sound system. Cinnamon wafted from burning incense in the center of the store. Even so, the place still smelled of ink and paper. Snacks, stuffed versions of the school mascot (the

Komensky Chupacabra), and merchandise imprinted with the school colors (yellow and green) surrounded the register. A coffee pot sat to the left side of the store. I bought a cup to warm my bones and turned back to Fannin.

"The book shelves are pretty picked over right now, but we're in the middle of the semester," he said. "That's normal. When the professors turn in their lists for next semester, the store will put in an order. As the new books come in, they ought to appear on the shelves."

"Ought to?"

He nodded. "They order the books and pay for them with district funds. After the books arrive, they remand them. Remand's when—"

"Yeah, when bookstores return books to the publisher for a refund." I sipped my coffee. It had cooked down too long, but the heat felt good.

"Right—only somebody here pocketed the refunds."

I looked around. "A small-town community college? How big could this be?"

"They've been running the scam a while. My troubles started when I made a three-and-a-half-million-dollar adjustment in the last financial statements."

"Yikes." A bigger deal than I had thought. "So what about the students who need books?"

"The store has to keep some books to sell, but they manage to rake off a bunch."

"Don't they have audits? Doesn't somebody reconcile sales, orders, and inventory?"

He gestured for me to follow. "Come on."

At the back of the store, Fannin led me through a door marked AUTHORIZED PERSONNEL ONLY. We took stairs descending into a basement. Unused display shelves, out-of-season holiday decorations, and boxed merchandise cluttered the room. In a back corner stood an unmarked metal door. I drank more of my coffee while he pulled out a key and led me through the doorway.

"Look around." He waved at the room. Rows of shelves of old books, floor to ceiling, filled the room and gave it a musty smell.

"What's all this?" I sneezed at the odor, sloshing coffee over the side of my cup and onto my trousers. *Damn.*

"A slush-pile. No auditor sees this room. These are out-of-date books, no value. When audit time rolls around, they borrow from this pile to balance what's upstairs. The auditors don't know one book from another. They just count 'em."

I paced down the rows of bookshelves, trying to get a rough mental tally. "Who's 'they'?"

"Don't know everyone, but the Chief Financial Officer has to be in on it." Fannin followed me. "He got himself in charge of the bookstore. Since then, he's come up with the cash to buy a good hunk of land alongside the river. Inside Rabb's Bend, northwest of town."

"Colorado River?"

"Yeah. Only river we've got. Peons like me don't get invited to the place, but it's supposed to be really something."

"How about the college president?"

"He's got to be. He approved the reorg putting the bookstore under the CFO, which is pretty strange. And he has the rest of the land inside Rabb's Bend. The story is, they both bought at the same time from an old rancher."

I nodded and kept walking. "What about the cops? Are they in on this?"

"Les Sobota, the sheriff, is big chums with the CFO. I've got no proof, but nothing else makes sense." Fannin paused and turned to me. "Sobota came to me when I started asking too many questions. I had

9

worked late, about ten p.m. When I got to my car, he came out of the shadows, swaggering with his thumbs stuck in his belt."

"The same personality as the one who stopped me. What'd he say?"

" 'I hear you're a busybody, Fannin,' " he mimicked. " 'That's not the path to popularity. I advise you to watch yourself. There's some lonely roads around here.' "

A voice boomed from the doorway: "I said it, but you didn't seem to get the message, did you?"

We both turned to the speaker. A burly cop aped the pose Fannin had just described. He stood close to my height—maybe five-foot-ten—but had a good thirty pounds on me. A military haircut and the gray of his eyes and hair cemented the hardness of his face, one that couldn't conceal the redness and wrinkles of a drinker. I caught a whiff of an alcohol fog from across the room.

"Morning, Sheriff," Fannin said. "Nacho, this is Sheriff Sobota."

"Good morning." I gave him my best fake smile.

The sheriff snorted. "Good morning, *shit!* There's a sign out there that says, 'Authorized Personnel Only.' Private Detective Nacho—yes, I know who you are—you got no call to think you're authorized." Sobota leaned forward and pointed a finger at Fannin. "And you. You sure as hell don't either. You've been reassigned. We don't cotton to people suing us." He waved his hand. "I ought to arrest you both for trespass, but who wants the paperwork hassle? Get the hell out. Now."

We walked to the door. Behind us, the sheriff called out, "One more thing, Mr. Private Detective Nacho. You got any more questions about things around here, you ask them to *me.* "

I turned back to face him. "Okay. You got a place on the river, too?"

He flipped me off. When I turned to walk away, he called out, "Hey, *amigo.* You go back where you came from." He paused and continued in a low voice. "Or you may find out more about that river than you want

10

to know. And Fannin, you've already had your last chance. This blows it."

*   *   *   *

Back under the canopy outside the building, I turned to Fannin and said, "It's lunchtime. Is there someplace we can get a bite and talk some more?"

He looked around. "We'll have an audience anywhere in this town. You head south on U.S. 77 to the Oakridge Smokehouse in Schulenburg. That'll put you closer to San Antonio anyway. I'll take FM 609, the road to Flatonia, and then cut back through Hostyn to get to Schulenburg. You'll have to wait fifteen minutes or so for me to get there."

I stayed at the top of the steps while he left in his car. A crow cawed in the distance, and the wood-smoke wafted toward me again. When I moved down the steps, my skin felt raw under the shifting of my clothes. Something seemed off.

I brushed it aside, fired up my car, and left.

Chapter 3: Buckners Creek

The Oakridge Smokehouse had a faux-country motif with an intentionally sagging red roof, vertical siding, and vertical trim at the joint of each board. The barbecue smelled great, even in the parking lot. My mouth watered.

Despite the luscious aroma, I ordered tea and waited for Fannin. The inside walls consisted of unfinished boards. Decorations leaned toward taxidermy and antique tools. Directly across from me, a jackalope—a jackrabbit mounted with small antlers—hung from the wall. I remembered seeing one on a meat-market wall as a child. My own eyes had seen it. It had to have been real.

Several families with small children sat scattered about the room. A toddler at the next table became dissatisfied with saltine crackers and squealed so we would all know. After a while, I eyed the scythe mounted on the wall just above him, not really wanting it to fall, but pondering what-if. My head throbbed from the uproar by the time his mother took him into her lap and gave him a bottle—tranquility, or as close as could be hoped for.

My watch said it had been forty minutes. I pulled out my phone and called. The cellular customer was not available. *Hmm.* I called Michelson and told him, "Fannin and I met this morning but broke up and agreed to meet for lunch in Schulenburg. He's a no-show." I gave Michelson the rundown on the morning, complete with the cops' attitude. He said he would see what he could run down from his end.

Another ten minutes passed. No Fannin. I ordered a brisket-and-pork-ribs combo platter. I stood at the register, paying my check, when Michelson called back: "Nacho, DPS reports a one-car accident on the route you said Fannin was to take. Head back up that way. See if it's not our boy they're fishing out of Buckners Creek."

It sounded ugly.

*　　*　　*　　*

It *was* ugly. Roadwork had slowed my progress, but I arrived in time to see a crashed car pulled back onto the bridge and up onto a tow-truck. I glimpsed first responders loading a bagged body into an ambulance. I parked and trotted to the scene. A DPS trooper held out his hand for me to stop. I showed him my private investigator's license.

"Officer, that may be my client. Is that Mark Fannin?"

"We can't release names until we've notified next-of-kin."

"Why didn't the guardrail keep him out of the creek?"

"We don't know yet. Near as we can tell, the rail had pre-existing damage, but if so, we hadn't gotten report of it."

"May I look at the car?"

"As long as you just look."

Looking told me all I needed. My stomach clenched so hard I almost bent over—it was the same make and model as Fannin's car, and the same license plate number. I pulled out my phone and took multiple pictures of the car, the bridge, the blown-out guardrail, and the road coming and going from the bridge. Whatever the inscription on the college administration building, the truth hadn't made Mark Fannin free.

A bulldozer sat nearby, a good mile from the rest of the construction. Its blade had bits of blue paint—the same color as Fannin's car. I got shots of that, too.

Butterflies, rainbows, and "I love you Daddy" flashed in my head.

Chapter 4: J. Thomas Fannin

I stared at the wall of my apartment. The complex, located on Broadway just north of downtown, sat on the former Smith Chevrolet site. For the money, you would expect the balcony to have a better view than a dog-park and a freeway ramp, but you would be wrong.

The pictures in Fannin's office crowded my mind—those photos and images of my daughter Kathy. My throat thickened, and my eyes squeezed to fight back tears. *Why haven't we talked in so long? How do I let myself get that busy?*

My phone lay on a side-table, seeming to look back at me. *She's busy, too. What if she's too busy to take my call?* My hand reached for the phone and paused. *What if she still thinks what she said when her mother died?* Kathy accused me of choosing the Corps over wife and family. I hadn't intended that, but maybe she was right after all. I had played drill-instructor for too long. Sometimes I would sit in the drive at home, struggling to turn off the D.I., and revert to husband and father. It had been hard to flip a switch.

And then the long deployment to Afghanistan, the nightmares when I came back, and the drinking to dull the pain. It had taken me years to get that under control. Mostly.

I paced and stared out the window, inhaled deeply, picked up the phone, and dialed.

"You have reached the voicemail of Kathryn Perez. I'm sorry I'm not here to catch your call, but please leave a message. Thanks."

"Kathy, it's Dad. Nothing urgent. We just haven't talked in a while, and I thought of you. Take care."

Back to sitting and staring at the wall. After turning on some Louis Armstrong, I allowed myself one shot of bourbon.

*　　*　　*　　*

A week after the crash at the bridge, a secretary handed me a cup of coffee and ushered me into the office of J. Thomas Fannin, Mark's father. J.T. Fannin Enterprises occupied a quarter of the twenty-second floor of a downtown San Antonio office building. Fannin Sr. had stepped away, so I sipped the coffee—good java this time, with a hint of coconut. I tried not to spill any of it on the intricately patterned rug, which looked like a real Persian. Probably Bokhara. My wife had liked these rugs. On my salary, she had to admire them from a distance.

The floor-to-ceiling corner-office windows showed me a panorama of the city. Large cylinders of rolled paper stood in a rack in the corner—GEOLOGICAL SURVEYS, the label read. The desk lay clear except for a pen-set, a model of a wooden derrick, and a pipe-tobacco-scented candle. I smiled and inhaled.

Old man Fannin stepped in. He stood tall and erect and made direct eye contact as we shook hands. He moved to his seat and appeared to note my glancing at the candle. His eyes twinkled. "The bastard building managers won't let me smoke in my own damn office, but they don't have a rule against candles."

We chatted briefly, and his face turned serious. "It's not over, Nacho. Killing Mark ended the whistleblower suit, but this isn't over until I'm done with these people, And right now, I'm a long way from done."

"What do you want Michelson and Associates to do?"

"I want these bastards brought down. All of them." He leaned forward and looked me in the eyes. "The whole rotten system, I want it down. And I want you and your agency to do it for me. I know how these systems work. They take advantage of people who can't fight back. But they screwed up when they killed my son. I can fight back. I can pay, and I don't care how you do it. I just want these people brought down—and preferably dead." Tears trickled down his face.

When clients ask you to break the law, it's best to sidestep. If you tell them "no," they may hire someone else. And I wasn't about to tell him "yes." I didn't want to lose my license, much less do time. "I can't promise they'll all end up dead, but Michelson and Associates is your best bet to bring these guys down. We've got depth, and we've got determination. We'll be glad to take the job."

He nodded, eyes still glistening. "Go after them. I want them hurt like they hurt me."

I hoped that getting people prosecuted would be good enough. It didn't occur to me that I might *not* find it good enough.

*　　*　　*　　*

Back at the office, I called Billy Amos, a DPS sergeant, to find out the status of the investigation into Mark's death. Amos worked in Austin. After pulling the file, he called me back: "Headquarters told us to stand down, that the local authorities would handle it."

"Do you know how I could find out the status of the investigation?"

Amos snorted. "The investigation's over. The final report says, 'Automobile accident.' "

I cocked an eyebrow. "Come on! There hasn't been time for a final call. And the circumstances are fishy as hell. What about forensics?"

"Forensics? Naïveté isn't good in a private detective, Nacho. Don't tell me you've never heard of the King of Komensky."

"The *what?*" I put my coffee-cup down and leaned forward.

"Martin Janak, the Komensky County Judge. It's spelled J-a-n-a-k, but the family pronounces it 'YAH-nak.' He's the king. He owns most of the politicians in the county. There'll be no forensic examination. Not now. Not ever."

"I don't care about some hick hotshot. How can they not investigate a death like this one?"

After a few moments of silence, Amos offered to meet me for dinner in a couple of days. "Some things are better discussed in person."

*　　*　　*　　*

Amos and I settled on a location between Austin and San Antonio: the Saltgrass Steakhouse on Sessom Road in San Marcos, just below the headwaters of the San Marcos River. On the outdoor patio, we could hear the river fall over a small weir. That and the redolence of sizzling steaks made for a pleasant ambiance.

After finishing my steak, I leaned back and took a deep whiff of the night air. It was fresh, and slightly cool. I could smell the moisture from the river. This signified winter in Texas, when you had to switch from a coat to short-sleeves from one day to the next.

When Amos swallowed his last bite and leaned back, I picked up where we left off: "How can they not investigate a death like this one?"

He pinched his lips together, pointed an index finger at me, and spilled out his words: "Every level of Komensky government is enmeshed in the Janak family business. When you think of Martin Janak, think of the Parr family in Duval County. Martin's cousin Lewis is the mayor. Martin's college buddy, Ruben Samaniego, is college president. Martin's brother-in-law, Thomas Czerny, is college CFO. Everybody in any position of power is a sibling, cousin, uncle, in-law, or something. It's an incestuous cesspool." His face twitched as if he had just realized his own wordplay. "The family's grip's so tight, state authorities haven't been able to penetrate his machine. Just like George Parr obscured goings-on in Duval County with a mesquite curtain, people say Komensky County's locked behind a pin-oak curtain."

I shifted in my chair. I knew the Parr machine only too well. My grandfather had been an enforcer for George Parr, keeping people in line—especially Latinos—and taking care of those who got restive, often with a bullet. "So we're going where the Rangers haven't gone?"

"Is that a problem?"

A chill breeze pierced my shirt. "No, just want to be clear what I'm getting into."

He tilted his head and looked me in the eyes. "A snake-pit."

We sat silently for a moment. College students at the next table laughed. The drawings by Fannin's children surfaced in my mind again. And then the shame of what my grandfather had done. Maybe this was a chance to make amends.

"I'd best get cracking," I said. "They've missed a bet if the bridge railing's not already fixed."

"Yeah, but give the pictures you took to an expert to see what he can make of it."

"Do you think I could get the expert access to the car?"

Amos laughed. "Nacho, think about what I've just told you. The car's already been through a crusher."

I gulped the last of my coffee, stood up, and leaned over the rail above the river. "If Fannin ran his car into the bridge railing, you'd expect the side colliding with the railing to be smashed, but the other side ought to be okay. In fact, both sides of Fannin's car got smashed—*really* smashed. My pictures show that. What's the authorities' story on that?"

Amos took in a deep breath, letting it go only after a pause. "They say the car's horizontal angle turned as it went over the bridge, and the other side smashed on the creek bed."

"Is there debris or paint on the rocks, or anything else to back that up?"

"It's not a rocky area, and we've had a lot of rain recently." Amos leaned forward, putting his elbows on his knees. "The creek's been up and down two or three times since the wreck. Even if the wreck left debris, it's probably long gone."

"Do you know anything more about these guys—Janak, Samaniego, and the crowd? Even something small I might find helpful later?"

Amos shook his head. "Not much." He leaned back and shrugged. "The file does say they're all a bunch of Aggies, sort of an A&M mafia. And Samaniego's supposed to be a clean freak. He wants everything spotless. They say you could eat off the hood of his car."

"What about families?"

"Most of them are married, I think. Except Ruben Samaniego. His wife died, and his kids are grown. I'm vague on details for the rest."

We talked a bit more. I stood, pulled down the back of my guayabera to be sure it still covered the .45 holstered in my waistband, and turned to the door. Amos raised a finger, catching my eye. "Are you really up for a snake-pit?"

I looked back at him. "Do you suppose these boys ever read Kipling?"

His eyebrows furrowed.

"Think of me as a mongoose, Rikki-Tikki-Tavi."

Chapter 5: Stonewalled

The guardrail at Buckners Creek had been repaired. I parked just beyond it and stumbled and slid down the steep, muddy slope. Even in February, a bright sun cast deep shadows under the bridge. Despite the chill on my previous visit, sweat made my shirt stick to my back. A concrete apron covered the area immediately under and around the bridge. When I got to a mud-coated apron, my feet slipped, and I fell on my rear. No harm done beyond muddy trousers, but getting back up the slope would be a bitch. And I certainly shouldn't have been wearing a new pair of dress shoes.

The muddy water flowed fast and obscured anything underneath. Poison ivy and Macartney's Rose, an impenetrable mass of thorns, sprawled over the banks. Dew soaked my cuffs. Dampness and the stench of rotting plants filled the air. A dead cedar branch helped me to stabilize myself and to poke around in the vegetation looking for something, anything that might prove relevant. No luck. About to cash it in, I caught a glint on the opposite side of the creek.

The branch also helped me to climb back up the slope to cross the bridge. I got down the far side without falling and cast my eyes about. What happened to the glint? I tried to retrace my line of sight from the opposite bank and find what had gleamed. No luck. Where was it? I moved down closer to the creek. One of my mud-caked soles slipped, nearly dumping me in the creek. Leaning forward, almost on all fours, I caught an oak-root protruding from the bank, pulled myself as far up as the root would take me, and cast my eyes about for something else to grab.

There—just below a small drop lay a car's side mirror—the glint. Macartney's rose obscured the mirror from above. No wonder the authorities didn't find it. And since they crushed the car, this was probably the only thing left.

I pulled against the base of a sapling to bring myself up to where it lay. Just as I grasped the mirror, the sapling gave, and my foot slipped. I

21

needed both hands to keep from sliding into the creek. Not willing to risk losing my prize, into the creek it was.

Hijole. The creek didn't quite reach my crotch, but it felt cold, and my footing nearly gave way in the strong current. With my free hand I grabbed an exposed tree-root and regained my balance. I worked, inches at a time, to a spot with better purchase for my feet.

I tossed the mirror into a safe spot and scrambled out of the creek. A few more roots and saplings helped me to climb the muddy slope to the highway, mirror intact. Mud caked my trousers, and my shoes were shot. *Damn. Still early morning.* I hoped for the day to get better.

The mirror's color matched that of Fannin's car. It was the left mirror—the authorities said his car landed on its right side.

*　　*　　*　　*

A quick trip back to the Executive Inn in Schulenburg let me change clothes, but squishy shoes had to do. Then it was back to the accident scene to look for witnesses.

Two residences had a view of the bridge. The first was a forlorn, faded house trailer in a weedy pasture, dated from when manufacturers' idea of charm ran to two-tone paint and a stepped roofline. A rusty washing machine sat abandoned to the side amid old tires and a wheel-less child's bicycle. A satellite antenna protruded from the roof. Three dogs of indeterminate breed barked from the pasture but didn't seem interested in stopping me from going to the trailer. No one answered the door, so I stuck a business card in the jamb.

The second residence was a small wood-frame house with peeling blue paint and plants hanging from the porch. A recently cut lawn graced the front. In contrast to the ruts leading to the trailer, a smooth gravel drive led to an aluminum carport.

An elderly black woman came to the door, with a Chihuahua yapping beside her heels.

"Good morning, ma'am," I said. "My name's Ignacio Perez. I'm a private detective looking into a one-car accident that happened on the Buckners Creek Bridge a while back. I was hoping—"

"You talkin' 'bout that college fella?" The dog kept yapping. She looked down. "Shush now, Bitsy." The dog didn't shush.

"Yes, ma'am. Mark Fannin. Did you by any chance see—"

"Fannin, right. No, I don't know nothin' 'bout that." She started to shut the door.

"Please. Do you know anyone who may have seen something?"

"No, can't say as I do."

She nearly had the door closed when I called out, "Please let me have your name so I can mark it off my list." I figured she would probably respond better to my telling her that I was crossing her name off a list than that I was adding her name to one.

The door stayed open a few inches, and she peered at me, as if to consider the downside of giving her name. "Mrs. Thibodeaux."

The door closed, damping the dog's yapping. But its volume increased as she cracked the door open again. "Listen here. You tell anybody who asks that I don't know nothin' 'bout this, y' hear?" The door closed again. I wedged a business card behind the trim and left.

She had given a damned good imitation of someone who had been warned not to talk.

Or maybe the real thing.

*   *   *   *

I sat in my car and considered my next move. Nobody had come home to the trailer, so I pulled onto the highway and headed to Komensky. Construction equipment still lined the road, and three men in hard hats leaned over plans spread over the hood of a pickup. I parked on the shoulder, walked up to them, and asked for the person in charge.

23

A middle-aged man of average build stepped forward. "That would be me, Carl Freeman." Thick glasses distorted his eyes, and something bulged under his lip. He turned and spat out a wad of snuff.

I introduced myself, began the spiel I had started with Mrs. Thibodeaux, and held out a business card. Freeman ignored it and interrupted me. "The guy who stirred things up at the college district—is that who you mean?"

"Yeah, that's the guy. Your work zone includes the bridge. I'm hoping someone here might have seen at least some of what happened."

"Nope. Not a thing." He spat again.

The other two men looked down but nodded their heads. One of them scuffed the grass with his boot. I lowered my hand with the card. "Well, I'm not too surprised that none of y'all saw it, but maybe some of your workers saw *something.*"

"Nope. Nobody here saw a thing." Freeman stared me in the eye. I stared back in his.

One of the other men kept looking down, and the third developed an intense interest in his cellphone.

"Even so," I said, "when your workers show up, how about if I ask them myself?"

The guy with the phone tried to be coy about snapping my picture. I hoped for his sake that coyness wasn't part of his job description.

"We got a schedule to keep," Freeman said. "You can't be hassling my workers. You stay away or answer to me."

"Clear enough." I turned to Phone Man. "Did you get a good enough shot, or do you want me to pose and smile?"

He shrugged and put his phone back in his pocket.

I turned to face the group. "A friendly county you got here."

24

As I headed back to my car, Freeman called out, "Don't count on it."

*   *   *   *

When I got to the outskirts of Komensky, my cellphone rang. I didn't recognize the number, but it was the voice of Mrs. Thibodeaux.

"Mr. Perez? You talk to Tommy Araya. He owns Tommy's Tacos. If something happens in this town, he knows about it."

Hot dog. "Thank you, Mrs. Thibodeaux. Is there anything else you can tell me to steer me in the right direction?"

"I told you what I have to say." She hung up.

Tommy's Tacos sat a block farther in from where I took the call. A blue polyethylene tarp spread over part of the roof, a letter was missing from the sign, and the old battered trucks in front told me the patrons would be light on movers-and-shakers. The tables were small, with metal legs and tops covered with linoleum that had long seen better days. Likewise, the chairs had lightweight metal legs screwed to plastic seats and backs. But I liked the *carne guisada* and the cute waitress. Young, she didn't look twice at me. The guy at the cash register seemed about my age, and I took him for Tommy.

"Good food," I told him.

"Thanks," he said.

"Are you Tommy Araya?"

"Last time I looked in the mirror."

I laid a business card on the counter and pushed it toward him. "Remember when Mark Fannin died a week or so ago? He's supposed to have wiped out on Buckners Creek Bridge. You know anything about that? Or of anybody who does?"

Tommy's face twitched just before his expression turned to stone, and he slid the card back toward me. "Nope, don't know anything about

25

that." His voice was loud. Then he lowered it. "And you're not going to find anybody who does."

I laid a ten-spot over my card and pushed them both toward him. "I'm beginning to notice that. How come?"

He looked around the room. "We got to live here."

I followed his gaze and saw several people watching us. Coldness descended on my stomach.

"Don't know nothing," he insisted, returning to a volume the whole room could hear. He gave me my change and slid my card under the tray inside his cash register.

Chapter 6: Witnesses Come Forward

As I pulled out of the parking lot, I saw a uniformed officer leave the taqueria and head for his patrol car. Before I could make it three blocks, the officer flashed his lights and pulled me over. *Shit, they're doing it again.* I stopped on the shoulder and left my hands at the top of the steering wheel as the officer approached. He was a deputy constable for Precinct Three. When he appeared at my window, I turned my head to face him, identified myself, and asked him for permission to retrieve identification.

"Yeah," he said, but he didn't look at what I gave him. "I'm Jorge Esquivel. It would be my job or worse if I'm seen talking to you, except like this, but we need to talk."

"Okay," I said. "How about Frank's Restaurant in Schulenburg at six this evening?"

"Done." He fiddled with his ticket-book and gave me a warning for inattentive driving.

*   *   *   *

I made it to the Fannin residence for my one-thirty appointment. With its brick exterior and size—probably three bedrooms and two baths—it fit right into the neighborhood, one of Komensky's nicer ones. I walked up to the front door with my satchel and knocked. Childish bickering came from somewhere inside.

A plump, attractive woman in her thirties came to the door. She matched the photo from Fannin's office. She wore makeup, probably for the occasion, and a nice dress, nicer than what I figured most women wore around the house. But she had on rubber gloves, a sign she wasn't quite ready for visitors.

"Mr. Perez?" she asked as she brushed stray hair from her face with her right-hand wrist.

"Yes, but call me Nacho, please."

"Sure. I'm Suzette." She looked down at her hands. "Everything was fine, and then the cat threw up."

I smiled. "They do that."

She directed me inside and motioned to a chair. While she tended to the cat's gift, two small girls looked at me soberly. "I'm Chloe," the older one said. "She's Emily." Emily bobbed her head and clutched a stuffed rabbit.

"Are you going to find out who killed my Daddy?" Chloe asked.

I caught my breath. The kid got to the point.

They both stood silently, looking squarely at my face. My heart melted, and I squinted my eyes to stifle tears. "Yes," I said. "That's why I'm here." I hoped my tone didn't betray my doubts. After all, I hadn't made anything happen yet.

Emily spoke this time. "Mommy says the bad people don't want us here, and we have to move." She turned her young face up to me, showing me her wide, innocent eyes.

How to comfort the child and not lie? I hugged her and held her out, looking into her eyes. "Mommies usually know best about such things," I ventured, remembering how Michelson hadn't mentioned comforting small children of murdered fathers when he had first hired me as an operative.

Suzette stood in the doorway, dabbing her eyes with a tissue. She shooed the girls into another room. "Emily reminds me of my Kathy as a little girl. She still means the world to me."

"Does she live with you in San Antonio?"

The world seemed to slow down, and my suddenly scratchy throat made it difficult to talk. "No, she's grown and works for the railroad in Omaha."

Suzette smiled, and I moved on to business. "Did your husband have any medical conditions or take any medication that might have caused him to lose control?"

"No." She shook her head. "The doctor recently told him to watch his blood pressure, but he didn't have any serious problems."

We talked about people Mark had worked with or had otherwise been close to. She gave me several possible leads, as well as a couple of thumb-drives with college records, which he had told her to keep in case something happened.

She put tissue to her eyes. "I thought he was being melodramatic."

I thanked her and put my notes and the thumb-drives in my satchel. Pausing, I glanced in the direction the girls had gone, and looked back at Suzette. "Emily said you're moving."

"We've got no ties here. And people's attitudes run from pity to disdain to worse." She paused and squeezed her eyes shut, more tears welling next to her nose. "I've been surprised at the hostility. Mark's actions must have threatened a lot of people. Maybe you'll be able to tell me how." She took a deep breath and dabbed her eyes again. "I had no idea how many the threat reached until they reacted."

Should have asked about this, too, dammit. Pulling my notes back out, I asked, "Tell me about the people with strong reactions."

She gave me names and positions of people, including community college administrators and numerous local business owners. "What surprised me and hurt the worst was Becky Freeman." Suzette looked down and back up at me. "Becky's kids are about the age of mine. We had play dates for them, and Becky and I worked on committees at church. We were BFFs, but she's turned cold, just shut me out."

"Would she be any relation to Carl Freeman, a contractor of some sort?"

She looked up and narrowed her eyes. "Yes, Carl's her husband. He owns the largest contracting company around here and does a lot of the public works projects. How do you know him?"

"Public works? Like highway expansion?"

"Yeah, sure, like that."

"I ran into him with a crew on the highway with the bridge and asked about possible witnesses. He brushed me off."

"That figures."

"How so?" I shifted in my chair.

"Mark became pretty skeptical about all levels of government around here. He never saw the contracting books, of course. But he told me skimming was a way of life."

"Did he share that with anybody besides you?"

"Not that I know of." Her eyes seemed to become unfocused. She looked back at me. "A few weeks ago, we spent some time with his parents in San Antonio. One afternoon, he took off for a few hours. I couldn't get a straight answer about where he'd been. But when doing the laundry, I found an FBI special agent's business card in his pocket."

"If word of that got back, it might have been enough to get him killed."

"How could it possibly have gotten back?" she asked.

"Who knows? An FBI mole seems unlikely, but it's something to think about."

She nodded. "Well, if Mark started something over contracting, that would explain Becky—" Her voice broke. "That gives a lot more people reason to have wanted Mark dead."

*　　*　　*　　*

30

A Dairy Delite drive-in sat across the street from the campus. I went to the window, got a cup of coffee, returned to my car, and called the people Suzette had listed as friends. Most didn't answer, and most of those who answered didn't want to be involved. But Emma Rosales, Mark's secretary in the accounting department, gave me a much-needed break.

"Yes, Mr. Perez, I want to help, but we can't be seen together, not even your car outside my house. But you're from San Antonio, right?"

"Yep."

An incoming call beeped in my ear. I ignored it to keep the conversation going.

"My sister lives in Floresville. We're visiting her this weekend. Could we meet then?"

At last—somebody who'll talk. "Sure. Floresville's no problem."

We agreed to meet at one o'clock Saturday at the Bill Miller barbecue in Floresville. Rosales hung up, and I checked my voicemail for the call that had beeped at me. "Dad, it's me, Kathy," went the message. "I'm sorry I missed your call and should have called you sooner. Things have been crazy for me, but there's big news, so please call me back."

Oh, boy. Big news had to relate to some guy. Well, she was 26. I had known I would hear that sooner or later.

I had just pressed the button to return her call when lights blinked in my rearview mirror. Sheriff Department's Car 13. *Good grief. Barney Fife again.* I killed the call.

"Step out of the car, Mr. Private Detective Nacho." He had me assume the position again, and he patted me down. "Whoa, Nelly. What's this?" He pulled out my .45.

I rolled my eyes. "Just what it looks like."

"Mr. Private Detective Nacho, you're supposed to tell me about this and your permit. But you didn't, and that's a serious matter."

31

"I'm supposed to tell you when you ask for my ID, but you haven't done that yet. Instead, you started off calling me the special nickname you made up. That made me think you remember me well enough from last time. And you saw my permit then."

"Look here, Mr. Private Dick—that's shorter. I'll go for that." A Cheshire-cat grin engulfed his face. He rocked back and forth on his feet. His wit seemed to please him. No accounting for taste. "I'm worried about you, Dick. I'm beginning to think you're not too bright. I don't see how you can solve cases when you're stupid, and by now you should've figured out we don't want you around here. If you haven't done that, you've got to be stupid."

"I'm supposed to guide my life by what you want?"

"Only if you're smart, Dick. And we've established that you ain't that." His eyes twinkled. "Here's a little something to make you ponder your welcome." He pulled out his ticket-book and started writing.

"What's my offense?"

"Burned-out taillight."

"My car's been parked and the engine shut off since well before you pulled up. You can't know anything about my taillight."

"Tell it to the judge."

"Your cousin?"

"No, Sobota's." His Cheshire-cat look came back, and he handed me the ticket. "And let me tell you one more thing, Dick." The last word carried a sneer. "You're not the only detective around. You'd be surprised what we know about you." He tossed my .45 onto the driver's seat.

"There's not much to know, pal. My life's pretty quiet. When cops don't give me tickets, that is."

Bruhn snorted and turned to leave, but reversed the motion. "You'll find out what we know the hard way."

32

Glancing at the ticket, I saw that the guy critiquing my intelligence had spelled it "taillite." I snorted and called Kathy back. *Voicemail. Damn.*

*   *   *   *

Frank's was filled with the odor of comfort food. The meatloaf special was adequate, if not memorable. Esquivel had the same, and topped his off with lemon-meringue pie. The din of conversation and clattering dishes kept our conversation private.

"What can I do for you?" I asked Esquivel.

"It's more what *I* can do for *you.* I know you're getting nowhere fast, and I know why." He chuckled. "It's like the mafia there, man. Nobody can talk about nothing. If they do, bad things happen. Sometimes people end up dead, like Fannin did."

"You didn't get your job by being on the political outs. How come you want to help me?"

"The constable owed my brother-in-law a favor. Besides, I got a Purple Heart in Afghanistan, and even County Judge Janak made a big deal of it."

I nodded. "Afghanistan's a bad place."

"No shit. Anyway, they got a lot of good will by seeing that I got a job."

"Okay, that explains the first part."

"The second part—yeah. My kid brother Rudy. He was fifteen years younger than me. He OD'd a while back. I want to get the bastards who did that to him."

"So who's that?"

"The Janaks. They control everything. Instead of fighting the drug-dealers, they cut a deal with them. The machine gets a piece of the action, and nobody gets busted."

33

"Drugs?" *Damn. This place is worse than I thought.*

"Everything, man, everything. Nothing happens here without the Janaks' say-so. Drug sales. Prostitution. Gambling. Killing your man Fannin. Nothing."

"Tammany Hall had nothing on these guys."

Esquivel tilted his head. "Huh?"

"Never mind."

"Okay, look, here's what I'm thinkin'." He offered to keep his eyes and ears open and give me the closest thing to an insider's view I was going to get. It sounded like a good deal—better than I had had before.

After dinner, I headed back toward Buckners Creek to see if anyone was home at the trailer. When I got close enough to see a car parked near it, I was pleased. Then I saw that the car belonged to the Komensky County Sheriff's Department. Car 13. Bruhn wasn't getting a big share of the graft.

*   *   *   *

At the Floresville Bill Miller's, I got a brisket plate and found an empty table in the back corner. Being thirty minutes early gave me plenty of time to sip syrupy iced tea and contemplate the red-brick walls and the cowboy motif, as well as the mixed lot of workmen and families that made up the clientele.

My phone lay quiet. Still no call back from Kathy, despite my having left three more voicemails since being in Komensky. I reached for my phone to call her again when a woman in a blue blouse entered and surveyed the room.

Emma's blue blouse and my guayabera were our agreed way of recognizing each other. I stood up, and she approached me and held out her hand. "You're Ignacio Perez."

A statement, not a question. We shook. Then she went through the cafeteria line to get food. When she got back, we talked. "Mark was a nice man," she said. "He didn't deserve to be killed."

I tilted my head toward her. "So the word on the street is murder?"

She put down her fork and looked me in the eye. "Of course." She raised and dropped her shoulders. "Most won't say so directly. They're too afraid."

"When's the last time you saw Mark?"

"We hadn't spoken since a few days before he died. Even then, we just ran into each other in the hall, asked about each other's family, that sort of thing. We hadn't seen each other regularly for over a month—not since they reassigned him."

"Who might know more about Mark's death?"

"Besides the sheriff's office, I'm not sure."

"Sheriff's office? Why them?"

"The day you and Mark met at the college, the day he died, I needed to deliver some papers to an office near the entrance. The two of you stood on the front steps when I went into the office. Coming out, I couldn't see Mark, but I figured he was just out of view. Wanting to say, 'Hello,' I walked over. Mark was already in his car and pulling away. After you headed to your car, Bruhn stepped from behind a column and into my view. He made a phone call. You couldn't have seen him, but he could hear you."

I slammed my fist on the table. *"Soy un imbécil!"* Leaning back, eyes closed, I turned my head from side to side in disgust. *Of course. How the hell else could they have known Fannin's route?* "Did Bruhn see you?" I asked Emma.

"I don't think so. Why?"

"You could get in trouble over this—or killed."

Her eyes fluttered, her face blanched, and she sat still for a moment. "No, he didn't see me. If he did, well, sometimes Mark brought his little girls into the office—" Her voice cracked and trailed off. Water seeped from her eyes. "Screw the bastards. Do what you have to do."

*　　*　　*　　*

I sat in the bright-white, well-maintained pergola on the Komensky town square. My cigar drowned out any other smells—a Rocky Patel *corojo,* it smelled good to me. I pondered my next move while gazing at the bright blue sky and the small children laughing and squealing on playground equipment—children surely oblivious to Komensky's rot. *Lucky for them.*

My cellphone rang. "Mr. Perez?"

"Yes."

"My name's Tommy Araya, owner of Tommy's Tacos, where you ate a while back. You left your card."

Hot damn. "I remember. How can I help you?"

"There's somebody you need to meet."

"Where and when?"

"How about tonight at my restaurant? Come to the back. We close at nine. By ten-thirty, everybody should be clear. Is that okay?"

"I'll be there." *Hallelujah.* This promised to be the break I desperately needed.

*　　*　　*　　*

Covering my tracks took me back to my motel in Schulenberg in the late afternoon. At ten-thirty-five that night, my car came slowly down the street. The dark taqueria looked abandoned for the night. No headlights from other traffic showed in either direction. I pulled behind the restaurant, sat, and waited. Nothing happened, so I got out, felt to assure my .45 sat securely in its holster, and knocked on the back door.

The door opened slightly, and Tommy Araya peered out and looked around. Apparently satisfied we had no watchers, he opened the door wider and motioned me into a dim kitchen.

A red security light provided the only illumination. A third man sat on a stool beside a stainless-steel-topped table. His completely gray hair and weathered face made him seem older than I, but his air told me life had been hard for him. We could have been close to the same age.

"Mr. Perez," Tommy said, "this is Florencio Narvaez. He's a heavy-equipment operator. He worked for Freeman Construction the day Fannin died. His dozer sat a few hundred yards from Buckners Creek. Florencio, tell Mr. Perez what you know."

Florencio nodded and looked at me. "You can't tell nobody we talked, right?" he said in heavily accented English. "I've got wife and family, you know. They depend on me. Nobody can know, right?"

I gave Florencio my most earnest look. "Nobody will know. It's just that everybody's stonewalling this, and leads are hard to come by."

Florencio sat silently and stared at me. I could see him sizing me up. He blinked rapidly, looked down, and rubbed the back of his neck. "Okay—see, I drive a bulldozer that day. I liked the project, you know, several weeks' work. But the boss come up to me and says to take the rest of the day off, full pay, you know?"

"By 'boss' you mean Carl Freeman?"

"Yes, Carl Freeman." He nodded several times.

"What then?"

"Well, I take off."

"Okay, then what?"

He gave me a puzzled look, his eyes blinking rapidly and his cheeks inflating and releasing.

Tommy put his hand on Florencio's forearm. "*Dígale lo que viste cuando te marchaste.*"

"*Sí*," I said. "What you saw when you left. *Favor de dígame.*"

"*Pues*, when I drive away, I see the boss in the rear mirror. He start up the bulldozer and drive it toward the creek, you know, where the college guy got killed. I went past the creek, around the corner, and drove into the grass where the boss couldn't see me. The boss waited by the bridge. I got tired of watching and walked back toward my truck when a car drove toward the bridge. I heard a loud scraping sound and screaming. The boss pushed the car off the bridge with the bulldozer. I hurried home and told no one. Except my wife and the priest. When we heard about the man who died, my wife told me to talk to Tommy Araya, so I did."

No wonder Freeman acted like a dick when we talked. "With the car paint on the dozer blade," I said, "it had to be something like this."

*   *   *   *

Back at my car, I studied my surroundings before getting in and driving off. All seemed as before, except for the red glow of a cigarette in a car parked half a block away. I've often thought I should have confronted whoever it was. But it probably wouldn't have helped.

Chapter 7: The Machine Fights Back

The clerk at the Komensky County Appraisal District frowned when I walked in. She seemed especially unhappy at my asking her to see the tax maps. Her eyes narrowed, and her neck and shoulders tensed. "What's your purpose?"

"I'm a member of the public wanting to see a public record. How's that for a purpose?" I smiled, which didn't seem to make her any happier.

"There," she said in a tart tone as she pointed at large books shelved under a table across the room.

"One more thing. Do you know who I am?"

She licked her lips and gulped from a water bottle. "Everybody knows who you are, Detective."

I headed to the tax maps. The beeps of a cellphone being dialed reached my ears.

The index listed only a few Samaniegos, and it didn't take me long to find Ruben's river property—probably half a section, and a similar parcel lay adjacent to it. The adjoining tract's parcel number easily traced back to CFO Thomas Czerny.

The map on my phone matched easily with the tax map, and in less than thirty minutes I reached Ruben Samaniego's property, traveling on a wider, better drained, better maintained gravel road than most in Komensky County. And smoother—no bouncing and rattling down a washboard. The arch over Samaniego's gate displayed an elaborate iron cutout of a Texas A&M logo. I got out and took pictures. The lush pasture, deep blue sky and fluffy clouds made a fetching image.

A hundred yards down and on the other side, another elaborate gate reared: Czerny's place. When I turned to my car, a tunnel of dust in the distance moved down the road from town. It was traveling fast. *Company soon.*

I was snapping a picture of Czerny's gate when Deputy Bruhn skidded to a halt a dozen yards away, clambered out of his car, and drew his revolver. "I got your business card at my trailer!" he shouted. "Damned little good that did you!" He waved his gun to the side and back. "We already knew you're a slow learner, Dick, but this time it's cost you. Letting me catch you out here with no witnesses is pretty damned stupid." He squeezed off two rounds, cowboy style, without aiming.

Aimed or not, one whizzed past my ear. I dropped into the four-foot-deep muddy ditch at the side of the road, slid down the 45-degree embankment, and fell at the bottom. Mud caked my entire backside and left arm, but I had no time to worry about that. My .45 pistol at the ready, I hunkered against the bank.

Shit, my spare magazine's in the glove box. A lesson late for the learning. He had shot twice and probably had only six to begin with. My weapon had seven in the magazine plus one in the chamber. Keeping the advantage seemed the best plan for the moment. I already had too many problems to shoot a cop if it could be avoided.

But what if had a speed loader? Dammit, then him or me. Not me, if I could help it. "You'll never get away with this, Bruhn!"

Bruhn moved slowly to the ditch. "The hell you say! You'll be killed resisting arrest!" He reached the edge of the ditch and popped off another round that grazed my thigh. Burning and blood. *Damn.* I pressed my hand against the wound to staunch the bleeding. I would live, but my thigh hurt badly. I gritted my teeth and squinted to focus. Letting the pain distract me would have gotten me killed.

That last shot put him down to three rounds out of six. Maybe. He shot so freely, he must have had a speed-loader—or been a fool.

He put one foot down the side of the bank, and I aimed to hit near the foot he still had on the crest. The round must have come close, because he jumped, stumbled, and slid into the ditch. He called out in pain and grasped his right arm—his gun arm—with his left hand. He had hurt it in the fall. His revolver lay in the mud.

I scrambled to him, keeping my .45 aimed at his belly. He scooted back with my approach. I picked his revolver up with my handkerchief and threw it over the fence into Czerny's pasture. The goat wire would keep him from slipping through the fence to retrieve it, so the *pendejo* couldn't avoid confessing to having been disarmed.

My .45 kept Bruhn in the ditch while I climbed out, ripped the radio microphone out of his patrol car, slipped the car into neutral, and pushed it into the ditch.

Did he have a cellphone? I hadn't found one in the car. Searching his person could have resulted in a fight. To end that, I might have had to send him to the hospital. Not a good idea with a cop. So if he had one, he kept it.

*   *   *   *

I patched up my wound with alcohol and drugstore bandages. Seeing a doctor would have raised too many questions. That done, I called Michelson, told him of my fight with Bruhn, and asked for standby legal assistance. I limped for several days while following dead-end leads and interviewing uncooperative witnesses. None of it led anywhere.

Why neither Bruhn nor Sobota confronted me was a mystery. Being arrested for assaulting a police officer seemed to be a sure bet, but it didn't happen. Still, only a fool would have thought the bastards had given up. They were cooking something up, surely. But it wasn't any fun waiting to find out what the dish was.

I pulled into Tommy's Tacos for lunch. The blue tarp still lay over the roof. A woman stood behind the register instead of Ben. Otherwise, it seemed to be the same noisy, busy place. I found an empty seat, and the cute waitress came over.

"Is your *carne guisada* good today?" I asked her. "It tasted great last time."

She put her pen to her order-pad and then looked up. Her eyes widened. Instead of taking the order, she hurried to the woman behind the register and whispered. The woman scowled, fumbled with her cash

41

drawer, stalked over, and threw my business card on the table. Her nametag said "Mercedes."

"Is that your card? You're Ignacio Perez?"

The room fell silent.

I looked up at her and nodded.

"How does it feel to barrel into a small town and ruin people's lives?" Her tears welled. "What goes through your mind to come back here? You want to gloat?" Her tears fell more freely, and she staggered. I leapt to my feet and slid a chair under her.

"You've lost me," I said, and took a seat next to her.

"They're dead." She glared at me with thin lips and hard eyes.

"Who's dead?" She baffled me.

"My husband Tommy and Florencio Narvaez. Murder-suicide, the cops say, but that's a lie. You killed them. You got them to talk about things that can't be talked about."

Heat flashed through my body, and sweat soaked the back of my shirt. I leaned forward and put my head in my hands. I sat silently, grinding my teeth, and turned to her. "*Madre de Dios*. I had no idea."

First Mark, and now Tommy and Florencio? This was the freedom the truth brought you in Komensky? My grandfather had done this sort of thing. I closed my eyes and took a deep breath. I couldn't let them see me shaken. Whatever I did would get back to the killers. I needed to put on a show, so I stood up and faced the room.

"I came here to help Mark Fannin, but this town killed him. I stayed on the job, and now this town's killed more, Tommy and Florencio." I paused for effect and swept my eyes across the customers' faces. "This isn't going to stop me. You tell the *pinches putos* that. Tell them they're coming down." I stomped out of the restaurant, feeling the eyes of the other patrons on my back.

42

The elevator doors opened on the top floor of the courthouse. Deep red paneling covered the opposite wall. Raised letters, trimmed in gilt, read MARTIN JANAK, COUNTY JUDGE.

"May I help you?" a receptionist chirped from a desk to my right. Behind her stood double doors, also lettered MARTIN JANAK.

I pointed to the doors. "Is that Janak's office?"

"Yes, but the judge is occupied at the moment. Do you have any appointment, Mr.—?"

"What do you think?" I strode past her and pushed open Janak's door. The man behind the desk looked up, eyes wide. The two people in front of his desk turned to me, one a pasty-faced man in a suit, the other Les Sobota, my second-favorite Komensky cop. His red face told me he had already been working on a bottle of whiskey.

I pointed at the man behind the desk. "Are you Martin Janak?"

His face reddened, and he stumbled over his words. "Y-yes. I am. I-I am busy now. Ask the receptionist for an appointment."

"The hell you say. I'm glad you've got Sobota here, because it'll save me the trouble of saying this twice. You bastards killed Mark Fannin, and now you've killed Tommy Araya and Florencio." I turned to Sobota. "You sent Bruhn to take care of me. It didn't work out. You shouldn't have sent a boy." I turned back to Janak. "You're coming down, you sorry son-of-a-bitch. You remember me, because when it happens, it will be because of me."

Sobota leaned back in his chair and smiled. "Judge, this here's the boy we was discussing, Private Detective Nacho Perez." He pulled a toothpick from his shirt pocket and stuck it in the corner of his mouth. "He's been troublesome of late, but no need to fret. We're already in the process of getting him under control."

I kicked his chair, making him fall backwards. Then I flipped him off, did the same to Janak, and stormed out of the room. The pasty-faced suit never budged or peeped.

Chapter 8: Omaha

Three days later, I had returned to my apartment in San Antonio. I leaned my chair against the wall on my balcony and closed my eyes. Freeway traffic and barking from a nearby dog-park drowned out Lightning Hopkins' guitar riff on my mp3 player. The deaths of Tommy and Florencio and my reaction swirled in my mind. I shouldn't have stormed into Janak's office, shouldn't have let them see me losing my cool. Bad form, and it made me seem weak. I needed to keep my mouth shut and focus on a big stick. Neither the Maker's Mark, nor my Cohiba cigar, nor the whiff of barbecue riding the pleasant breeze could fade Komensky.

I leaned forward and, on my laptop, scrolled through a copy of the documents from Fannin's thumb-drives. The accounting firm we had hired had told us the files warranted deeper investigation, but they were too dry and abstract for me.

Michelson called me on my phone. "Nacho, we've heard from the expert we hired to reconstruct the accident."

"What's the word?"

"Zip. He doesn't have enough to work with. Even the side mirror you got doesn't help. It's odd that it's from the left side, but he can't make anything out of it that would stand up."

"And I ruined a good pair of shoes."

Michelson chuckled. "Bill those to the client."

We hung up, and I leaned back with my cigar. The barking let up as Lightning Hopkins started "Mojo Hand." I closed my eyes and let the beat reverberate. The phone rang again. *No peace.* Michelson had probably forgotten something.

"Nacho here."

A throat cleared on the other end. "Is this the father of Kathryn Perez?"

My heart rate quickened. "Yes, Ignacio Perez, how may I help you?"

"I am Sergeant Molrova of the Omaha Police Department. I'm sorry to inform you that your daughter has been in an automobile, uh, incident." I should have picked up on the word choice, but the news had shocked me.

I dropped my chair on all fours and froze, my stomach in a tight ball. "Is—is she okay?" I asked, tripping over my words. *Not likely, since she didn't make the call.*

"She's in critical condition. You're listed as 'Dad' on her cellphone, and we didn't know who else to call. The doctors can't say more about her prospects, or about the baby's, either."

I gasped and slumped forward in my seat. "Baby? *What* baby?"

"Your daughter's about seven months pregnant, Mr. Perez. They had to deliver the boy with an emergency Caesarean."

Big news, she had said. I had figured that meant a guy, sure. But a baby had never occurred to me. Now I was a grandfather—if the baby lived.

"Did the baby make it?"

"So far, yes. He's in the NICU."

He gave me a contact phone number and the hospital address and room number. I left voicemails with Michelson and Old Man Fannin before booking a ticket on the first flight to Omaha. The immediate tasks done, I dropped my head to my knees and breathed deeply.

Critical condition.

A baby.

In the NICU.

46

God almighty. For the first time in years, I prayed. I didn't deserve to be a grandfather, but I never wanted anything as much as I wanted Kathy and the baby to make it. Face in my hands, I struggled to come to terms with having a grandchild—one who might not live until I could get there to see him. A hitch crept into my throat, but I forced it down and concentrated on keeping my breathing regular.

*   *   *   *

Bland-colored ceramic-tile walls with handrails and a patina of age were my first impression of the Omaha hospital. A low-level disinfectant smell permeated the air. The sounds were disorienting: ringing phones, paging intercoms, medical equipment alarms, nurses' aides bustling by with carts, and nurses chatting at their stations, their words inaudible in the low-level clatter.

I found Room 312 and entered Kathy's ward, a large room with multiple beds surrounded by curtains. The disinfectant seemed stronger, and the ambient noise lower. At one of the beds, several doctors whispered to each other. With a grim expression one of them pulled a sheet over the patient's face. My heart leapt into my throat, and my knees wanted to buckle.

A nurse, who must have seen me standing and staring with my mouth agape, asked, "May I help you?"

"Kathryn Perez. I'm looking for Kathryn Perez."

She pointed to a bed in the back corner. *The sheet wasn't for Kathy. Thank God.*

Needles with tubes stuck out of Kathy's wrist, arm, and neck. An array of medical equipment stood behind her; the displays were an incomprehensible parody of an early science fiction movie's computer. A heartbeat. Part of the display looked like a heartbeat.

The nurse gave me a few minutes with my daughter. "Why's that tube in her mouth?" I asked.

"She's intubated," the nurse said, "to help her breathe."

47

"Kathy? It's me, Dad."

"She probably can't hear you," the nurse said. "She's too heavily sedated. But it doesn't hurt to try."

Kathy had a swollen face with bruises all over. My breathing sped up. I squeezed my eyes to keep them from watering. The nurse left. I sat, holding her unusually warm hand and losing the battle with my tears. I whispered memories from her childhood.

My shoulder suddenly felt a tap. "Time to leave," the nurse said.

I squeezed Kathy's hand tighter.

"Sir, you really must leave."

I willed myself to my feet and leaned over, kissing Kathy's forehead and whispering in her ear, "*Mijita*, I love you."

Outside the room, I asked the nurse, "What are her chances?"

"The doctor should be back later in the afternoon. Ask him then. Her breathing and heart rate have strengthened. Take that as good news."

I did. I needed to.

The NICU was one floor down, at the other end of the block-long building, accessible only through a maze. Yet the fifteen-minute walk helped me to get ahold of myself after seeing my daughter. I trusted myself to the directions at each corridor intersection and missed only one, which cost me a few minutes of bewilderment.

Bright primary colors dominated the NICU waiting-room. Adults whispered among themselves and flipped through out-of-date magazines. Not caring about the Kardashians' exploits, I knocked on the door of the NICU itself. A nurse let me in. "Five minutes," she said.

NICU equipment made noise, too, but not as much as where they had Kathy. Across the room in the middle, I saw where her boy, my grandson, lay in an enclosed incubator. BABY BOY PEREZ, the label read. The nurse opened the front, but even so, I couldn't see much. His

48

eyes were shut, and he had a too-big head and brick-red wrinkly skin covered with a downy fuzz. A feeding tube protruded from his mouth and other tubes from his feet. A lamp shone down on the newborn.

I stared at him. I had given up on grandkids, but here this boy lay, hanging onto life only with the aid of machines. My eyes had dried on the walk from Kathy's room to here, but now water cascaded. My knees nearly gave. To keep from falling, I grabbed the table on which the incubator sat.

Stop it, dammit. Stop it.

I took a deep breath, held it and tensed my arm and chest muscles. Another breath. *Dammit.* I willed my body still and stood with my eyes shut. I stopped the tears, breathed deeply, and looked up. The nurse stood to the side, her eyes cast down.

Behind my grandson was more machinery similar to what ensconced Kathy—a confusing array of displays. Then I found what looked like a heartbeat, just as for his mother. I whispered to the nurse, "Is that his heart? It's so fast."

"Yes. Infants have rapid heartbeats. It's what you should expect."

"So it's good?"

"Under the circumstances, yes."

Under the circumstances. Not what I wanted to hear.

Chapter 9: It Gets Personal

The people in the hospital visitors' area sat, waited, and no doubt nurtured hopes much like my own. My jaw ached, and my chest was tight. Waiting sucked. Her car. Somebody needed to deal with that. Sergeant Mulrova's number was on a napkin in my pocket. He answered on the third ring.

"Sergeant, this is Nacho Perez, Kathryn Perez's father. We spoke yesterday. I'm here in the hospital, but this waiting and not doing is too much. What about Kathy's car? What can I do to help with it?"

"The impound lot has it, completely totaled." He cleared his throat. "Anyway, the car belonged to the driver, her fiancé, we're told."

Fiancé. She was engaged, and I didn't know. "How is he?"

"Didn't survive the crash."

I quivered. "Let me be the one to tell her. What was his name?"

"Benjamin McGinty. He worked at the Union Pacific."

"Same as Kathy."

"Listen, I've got some questions. Can we meet?"

"Sure." We settled on the hospital lunchroom in thirty minutes.

The lunchroom's function seemed to be drumming up business for the cardiac wing. Corn dogs, chicken wings, French fries, and other comfort food filled the menu. The odor of grease wafted through the air. My stomach growled and my mouth watered, reminding me I hadn't eaten since San Antonio.

A sign reading BIG RED had caught my eye—my favorite soft drink, but the logo didn't look right. I pointed to a cup and the sign. "A large Big Red, please."

They laughed. In Omaha, "Big Red" referred to the Nebraska football team, not the soft drink. A Coke had to do.

Mulrova strode in. We sat in the corner, him with a cup of coffee, me with a hamburger and chips. Mulrova studied his coffee and swirled it in the cup. He took a sip and looked at me. "Does your daughter have any enemies?"

I stopped mid-chew and stared at him in incredulity. *Enemies? Holy shit. He wasn't thinking 'accident.'* Washing the bite down gave me time to formulate a response. "We never discussed anything like that. So this wasn't an accident?"

"Mr. Perez, we don't think so. It looks like an eighteen-wheeler intentionally pushed her car off the Douglas Street ramp leading up to Interstate 480."

My eyes blinked. "An eighteen-wheeler. What makes you think it happened on purpose?"

He sipped his coffee. "The truck had been stolen that same day. Shortly after the incident, Council Bluffs P.D. found it left at an abandoned warehouse. Whoever took it had wiped it clean, prints and everything. We can't even find a hair." He took another sip, set his cup down, stared at it, and looked up at me. "And one more thing. The owner had secured the trailer with a heavy padlock. The cargo consisted of cold medicines that meth dealers would pay a pretty price for. When we got the truck back, nobody had tampered with the lock. They must not have cared about the contents."

"You're saying they stole the truck just to run Kathy off the road?"

"That's what I think."

My fists clenched as a cold fury washed over me. *Komensky. This is what Sobota meant about getting me under control. The bastards had used Kathy to get to me.*

"Do you have any idea why somebody might want to do something like that?" he asked. "Or who?"

Anger welled up within me. *"Hijos de putas.* That's why they didn't bring me in for assault. *Van a pagar."*

"Come again?"

"Thank you, Sergeant. You've told me what I need to know."

"Peachy, only I'm the police officer here. A moment ago you were worried about your daughter and grandson. Now you're pissed off. What's going on?"

I bit my lip and considered my options. "Kathy's being run off the road can't be a coincidence. I'm a private detective. This is tied in with a case I'm working on. How about a short rundown?"

Mulrova smirked. "No, give me the *Alice's Restaurant* version with five-part harmony and full orchestration." *So he likes arcane musical references. Me, too.* He got the version he wanted.

Two cups of coffee later, I finished, and Mulrova put his elbows on the table, shut his eyes, rubbed his temples with his fingers, and looked up. "Two murders by pushing vehicles off bridges. If the first one was a murder, that's your connection?"

"Yeah. Carl Freeman did the first. I'm betting he did this one, too."

He shook his head. "The link seems thin." He leaned back, rubbed the bridge of his nose, and blinked his eyes. "Man, I've seen some squirrelly stuff here, but you guys in Texas are really screwed up."

"We've got a long, proud history of corruption. Back in the time of World War I, the legislature impeached Governor Pa Ferguson and convicted him of corruption. Later he got his wife elected. Ma Ferguson promised the voters two governors for the price of one, because she'd follow her husband's advice."

"Texans." Mulrova rolled his eyes and looked back at me. "Who would be the best law enforcement contact in Komensky County?"

"Sergeant, remember what I said. There's nobody. They're all in on it."

*　　　*　　　*　　　*

The doctor turned to leave just as I entered Kathy's room. We shook hands. "Ignacio Perez, doctor." I pointed at Kathy. "Kathy's father. What can you tell me?"

The doctor looked at me and then down at his notes. "Let's step into the hall." We did. He looked down at her chart and bit his lip. "Look, she's stable. Her vitals are good, considering what she's been through— first the crash, then the Caesarean. Without considering those things, not so good at all." He flipped through the sheets on his clipboard. "You're her father. Can you tell me about her family?"

"Her mother's dead, and she's an only child, so I'm it." I said. "Except for the baby downstairs."

"So, with her fiancé dead, you'd be the one to take the baby if she doesn't make it."

A huge board slammed into my chest, knocking out my air. Some part of me had known this, but hearing it said it aloud made me confront it. My lungs gasped. "Yes." My voice croaked.

*　　　*　　　*　　　*

After a week, Kathy pulled through. I broke the news of her fiancé's death. She took it hard but seemed buoyed her baby's health. Named Benjamin after his father, he was a pink, squirming bundle of thirst. Propped up on pillows in her hospital bed, she nursed Benny. I had never seen her look so happy. For his part, Benny worked vigorously to get what he wanted. For a while we sat silently, so Benny's smacking noises were the only sounds in the room apart from the HVAC—so different from all of those monitors and other machines they had both been hooked up to. Life looked rosier than it had been in a long time.

"Kathy, have you thought about what you're going to do?"

Kathy leaned down and kissed Benny's head. "I'll go back to my apartment and work. What else?"

54

I glanced out the window. White everywhere. Some of the cars in the parking lot were entirely covered with snow, and it still fell. She couldn't live here alone with a baby. "Will you be able to handle him and your job?"

Kathy smiled at me. "Dad, I've got some leave built up, and the railroad offers good benefits. I'll be fine."

"He'll have to head right into daycare."

"Dad." Kathy exhaled a long breath. "This is my life. It'll be hard with a baby, but I wouldn't trade Benny for anything. Ben's being gone hurts, worse than anything. But we can't change that. Benny's as good a reason as it gets to go on."

My head dropped, and my eyes squeezed shut.

"My job's here, Dad. I can't just move back to San Antonio with no job and no insurance. Not with a baby. You know that."

I let out a long breath. "I don't have to like it."

Kathy looked into my eyes. "Are you going to be okay? That's what worries me. What are you going to do?"

"Oh, I've got plenty to do. The people who did this to you and Benjamin, they haven't heard the last of me."

"Not what I wanted to hear. Dad, please don't do anything stupid."

I took her hand, pressed it between mine, and looked her in the eyes. "You know what I did while you were growing up." I paused and looked her in the eye. "No better friend. No worse enemy. They may have heard it, but they don't feel it. They will."

"Dad, Benny and I are okay. That's enough. Please don't let anything to happen to you."

"What has to come, has to come."

*   *   *   *

I left my keys with the valet and walked up the steps to the San Antonio Country Club. I had switched my usual guayabera for a dress shirt, sports-coat and tie. Near the end of a wide central hallway, waiters bustled about. Large windows at the end of the hall offered a view of the golf course. Persian carpets lay on the hall floor, and the vases on the end tables probably didn't come from Sears.

When I neared the windows, a maître d' approached me. "William Fannin's party, please," I told him.

Fannin sat alone in a side room. "We'll be the only ones in here this afternoon," he said.

Good move. My eyes instinctively flitted around, looking for signs of a listening device. That was a futile gesture, for I saw nothing, which meant nothing, but the topic of conversation required me to trust him. So I did. I don't recall previously encountering such an elaborate array of silverware, but I watched what Fannin used when and did likewise.

Tomato consommé came as the first course. One taste, and I knew they hadn't served Campbell's.

Salad with vinaigrette came next. I couldn't name all the greens, but they weren't bad.

"Do you follow the Spurs, Mr. Perez?" Fannin took another bite of salad.

"Nacho, please. Sure, most of the time. Their chances look pretty good this year."

He smiled, chewed, and swallowed. "They do. Let's hope that bears out."

We chatted about the Spurs and San Antonio's chances for an NFL team until the waiter brought the main course and refilled our drinks. Fannin turned to the waiter. "Thank you. This will be all. We'll let you know if we need anything else." The waiter slipped out of the room.

I started to explain why I had wanted to meet, but he held up his hand. "Let's enjoy the food first."

We did. The smell of the filet of sole with cilantro sauce made my mouth water. I took and bite and savored it. "A remarkable dish."

He nodded. "That it is. Every time I've ordered it, I've been pleased."

During the rest of the meal we chatted more about sports and about which candidate in the upcoming mayoral race the Northside business community would support. After we had both slowed down, Fannin gestured toward me. "You asked for a meeting, Mr. Perez. That makes me assume this is something we should not discuss over the phone. Your reports stopped a while ago. Are we here to discuss that?"

"In part. The reports stopped, because I stopped." I paused, leaned back, and placed my palms flat on the table. "They went after my daughter in Omaha. That's where I've been. They ran her car off a freeway ramp. Her fiancé is dead, and she and my grandson nearly died."

Fannin's face remained impassive. I took a sip of wine, set the glass down, and leaned back. "This will not stand," I continued. "I need you to be clear what's coming down, and I need to know whether you're on board."

"Of course, I'm on board," Fannin said.

"Hear me out." I held up my hand palm out. "When we talked before, you said you didn't care how we brought them down. But I danced around that, because I didn't want to break the law. That's changed." He stroked his chin but said nothing, so I continued. "I intend to get the bastards to turn on each other, to take each other out. I probably won't personally pull a trigger, but so what? I'll set in motion things that get triggers pulled. And if I end up doing some shooting, so be it. Are you ready to go there? Either way, it'll happen. But your money will make it quicker and easier. Are you okay with that?"

He sat silently, looked me in the eye, and raised his eyebrows. After a moment, he lifted his wineglass to the light and swirled it. He took a small sip with his eyes closed. He swallowed and looked at me. "Entirely sufficient, don't you think?" He nodded his head.

"Yes, Mr. Fannin. Entirely sufficient." I, too, savored a sip of the wine.

An image of my grandfather came to my mind, but I brushed it away.

Chapter 10: Crossing the Line

I called the office and got Chuck Mahaffey, our electronics expert. He and Lamont Washington, another of our long-time operatives, put a team together. Photographs of county and college district maintenance workers enabled us to duplicate their uniforms. Within forty-eight hours of having the uniforms, we sent operatives into the offices of County Judge Martin Janak and College President and Ruben Samaniego on the pretext of maintenance. We bugged their offices and tapped their phones. Not worrying about warrants or probable cause made life easier than for cops. And the big expense account helped, too.

We set up a listening center in a former dentist's office. The landlord, happy to get six months' rent in advance in cash, didn't ask questions. We even had an extra room where one of us could snooze while another listened—except, instead of snoozing, Lamont would study Bible lessons.

* * * * *

I next needed to talk with Esquivel. He didn't want to meet in Schulenberg again. He was feeling heat and thought Schulenberg would be too close to Komensky. So we met another twenty miles away in Hallettsville. Even on a Tuesday night, the Jalisco Mexican Restaurant served a crowd. As with our previous meeting at Frank's, the ambient noise offered privacy for conversation. Food nearly overflowed the plate, and the aroma of salsa and enchilada sauce filled the air. Half my beans and rice remained on my plate, but Esquivel packed away everything he got, plus four flour tortillas. Maybe he needed to worry less about Janak's mafia and more about a heart attack.

When we were finished eating, Esquivel ordered a third Corona. I nursed a cup of coffee.

"I've got a new plan, Jorge, but I need your help."

He paused with his beer in midair. "In what way?" He put the beer back down. "The only reason I'm still kickin's because I keep my head down."

"You're okay with spreading gossip, *chisme*, aren't you?"

"*Chisme*? Hell, I do that anyway." He took a big gulp of Corona.

"Yeah, but this is different." Despite the high ambient noise, I looked around and then faced him, leaned forward, and lowered my voice. "How scrupulous are you, whether the *chisme* is true."

Esquivel grinned. "*Oye*. The best kind mostly ain't." He took another swig and chortled.

"Let it be known around town that Thomas Czerny, the college CFO, was seen in a San Antonio restaurant with a well-known criminal-defense lawyer and some federal prosecutors. Papers were all over the table, and Czerny seemed to be explaining the papers to the prosecutors. Think you can handle that?"

Esquivel leaned toward me and narrowed his eyes. "Where can I tell people I got information like that?"

"Hasn't somebody moved away to the San Antonio area in the last few years? Come up with something and stay as vague as you can. Say you don't know anymore, but tell at least a dozen people who'll probably pass it on. Let me know when you're done."

Esquivel nodded his head. "You trying to blow up the whole damn county?"

I put my hands on top of my head, rocked back in my chair, and mouthed, "Boom."

*   *   *   *

Waiting for a phone-tap to yield something useful can be tedious. Even crooks have routine business, and we weren't hearing anything interesting. We had spent three boring hours manning the tap, when

Lamont produced a deck of cards and pulled his cheeks back in a grin, eyes twinkling.

"Gin rummy? A dollar a point?"

Mi mamá had warned me about offers like that. "Hah. I've heard about you and gin rummy. No money if we play."

Not playing for money was my smartest move in a week. Lamont ginned three times for every time I did. The score was ugly.

"Nacho," he said, "some people just aren't born to play cards." He laughed and slapped me on the back.

Two days later, the Martin Janak tap hit pay dirt. Martin met with his cousin Lewis, the mayor, to discuss the Czerny rumor.

"Lew, do you think this is on the level?" That had to be Martin Janak's voice.

"It doesn't look good. I'm not one to leave loose threads."

Martin coughed. "Let me call our boy in the FBI."

We heard beeps as he dialed the phone. "Special Agent Conroy, please." There was a pause. "Marty, tell him Marty's calling. He'll know."

Another pause, and then Martin chimed back in. "Fair enough you don't like me calling you at work, but we've got a situation. There's a story that Thomas Czerny, the college district CFO, is cooperating in an FBI investigation. Find out if that's true, and find out *now.*"

There was silence, punctuated by Martin 'uh-huhing' and 'I-seeing.' Then he continued. "You need to do better than that. Why don't you go chat somebody up at the water cooler or something?" More 'uh-huhing' and 'I-seeing.' Then finally, "Well, all right, but be sure and let me know as soon as you learn anything more."

A phone receiver slammed. "That bastard," Martin said. "Conroy doesn't know. The office has a few confidential investigations. Only those with a need to know get information. So he can't say for sure. Makes you wonder what we pay him for."

Lewis jumped into the conversation. "We can't take a chance. We've got to act like the rumor's real. Who can we get to take Czerny out?"

Silence intervened. The bug picked up chairs creaking and papers being shuffled. Then Martin spoke: "Let's give Ruben a chance to deal with it first. My secretary called him, and he's sitting outside right now."

"Okay, if you think so."

The bug picked up a buzz and Martin Janak telling his secretary to send in Mr. Samaniego, the college president. We then heard a door open, and then footsteps. A new voice said, "Good morning, Martin, Lew." It sounded chipper.

"Have a seat, Ruben." I recognized Martin Janak's voice. A moment of silence followed. "Ruben, the grapevine's telling me things are getting out of control at the college."

"What do you mean? What have you heard?" The chipperness was gone.

"Your boy, Czerny. There's a rumor he's cooperating with the feds. If that's true, we're all in deep shit." The sharpness of Janak's tone came through the bug.

Samaniego responded quickly, but with a defensive tone. "That can't be true. Tom wouldn't do that."

"People do all kinds of things in a pinch. Is he in one?"

"Not that I know of."

"Well, find out, dammit. Convince me this is all bullshit, or I'm going to take care of it." The menace in Janak's voice came through clearly.

"Sure, Martin. Sure thing. I'll get right on it."

"See to it that you do." Janak's tone was chilling. The recording picked up the sound of a chair scooting, and Janak continued: "Ruben, you've got to run a taut ship over there, you hear? I can't have people under me letting things get out of control." He paused and lowered his voice. "If there's a problem, you need for me to hear about it from *you,* not some rumor on the street. You understand me? And I sure as hell don't want to be hearing about it from the FBI."

"Yes. Yes, I understand, Martin." Samaniego's voice quavered.

Esquivel had done his job, and we had confirmed a mole in the FBI. Things were cooking.

*   *   *   *

We mailed Martin Janak a Photoshopped image of Czerny sitting in a restaurant with dark-suited men and stacks of paper. The paper Czerny held up showed the college district's logo.

The day after that, I called Emma Rosales at home and asked about morale at work.

"There're rumors everywhere," she said. "People from the president's office are asking about Thomas Czerny, what he does with his time, where he goes, whether he takes any papers or computer things with him when he leaves. They even said he's talking to prosecutors. Could that be true?"

Letting her in on our plan was too risky. "You're on the scene, Emma. What do you think?"

"Maybe he is. Everything was routine, but now things are unraveling. Everything's gone crazy."

The phone call merited a celebration, two fingers of Maker's Mark, and another cigar, this time a Gurkha Red Witch. Mahaffey joined me with a beer, but as it was a Wednesday night, Lamont headed to a prayer meeting. He had adopted Bethlehem AME Church while we were in Komensky.

Chapter 11: The First Pin Falls

Later in the week, television news reported that a passerby had found Czerny dead on a remote county road, a single gunshot to his head. Les Sobota stood in front of cameras on the steps of the college district administration building. When they backed up for a longer shot, you could see the school motto about knowing the truth and it making you free. Czerny had gotten a taste of Komensky freedom.

Sobota projected a flat affect and spoke in a monotone as American and Texan flags flanked him. "The gunshot wound was self-inflicted. Our investigation has found evidence that Mr. Czerny was involved in improprieties at the college district. We are saddened for his family that Mr. Czerny saw no way out other than suicide, but we assure the public that we will continue to probe the improprieties and apprehend all who may be involved."

Ruben Samaniego stood behind Sobota, wiping perspiration from his forehead. *Self-inflicted, my ass.* Sobota's barrel would probably have still burned my hand if I had touched it.

After the news segment ended, Mahaffey clicked off the television, and we sat quietly for a moment nursing beers and digesting the news. "One down," I said. "Now we need to make something else happen."

Mahaffey took a swig of beer and pointed it at me. "That's easy enough. What about putting some heat on Samaniego?"

I nodded. "Samaniego next. That seems good. We ought to plant evidence on him and tip off Janak."

"On him or in his car?" Mahaffey asked. "Wouldn't his car be easier?"

Lamont gazed into the distance, so I chimed in. "If you could get in his car without setting off an alarm."

We stewed it over. I finished my beer and tossed the bottle in the trashcan beside the desk. A recollection hit me: "Neat freak. Billy Amos told me Samaniego's a neat freak."

The following morning, Lamont Washington put on a maintenance-worker uniform and swept the college-district lot where Samaniego parked. When he neared Samaniego's car, two other of our operatives, Angel Marrero and Chuck Mahaffey, started a shouting match fifty yards away. The distraction assured that casual bystanders wouldn't notice Lamont smearing Samaniego's car with a mixture of oil and dirt. Lamont worked a few more minutes, changed clothes in his car, and went to the only full-service car-wash in Komensky.

We watched Samaniego come back to his car at lunch. We were too far to hear his words, but from my limited lip reading they didn't seem suitable for mixed company. Fortune smiled on us, and he headed straight to where Lamont waited. I followed discreetly and watched the entertainment.

Lamont tugged the sleeve of a car-wash attendant and held out a small object, which I knew to be a thumb-drive. It had the college district financial records we had gotten from Mark Fannin's widow. Words passed between Lamont and the attendant. The attendant hesitated, shook his head, and turned away. Lamont spoke more, wrapped what looked like a bill around the object, and offered it again. *A Benjamin, no doubt.* The attendant paused, and more words passed between them. He tilted his head, grimaced, and pocketed the object.

When they finished Samaniego's car and he paid and drove away, the attendant walked up to Lamont, who slipped him more money.

*   *   *   *

That afternoon, Mahaffey used a burner phone to place an anonymous call to Martin Janak. I listened in. "You assumed Czerny was acting alone," Mahaffey said. "Assumptions are foolish. Have somebody check out Ruben Samaniego's car. He's sneaking out incriminating information."

"Who is this?"

"Consider me a friend doing you a favor, a second favor. That picture of Czerny was from me. Check Samaniego today, as soon as possible, or it may be too late."

"How the hell do you know this shit? Who are you—"

Mahaffey hung up the phone and took another swig of his Corona. He paused, squinted, and glowered at me. "We're working these guys over good, Nacho. You think that's right?"

Lamont shook his head. "Nacho, you know me. I'm with you on getting evidence on these snakes, but setting them up to be killed . . . That's dirty business."

I reached for Mahaffey's beer and took a swig myself. "Look at all the people they've killed, including my daughter's fiancé. They put her and my grandson in the hospital. Bruhn would have killed me out on that county road if I hadn't been armed. *They* set the stakes, not me. I'm just playing their game."

*   *   *   *

Carl Freeman seemed a good next prospect. I drove by his job site north of town and saw him giving directions to his crew. I called Mahaffey, told him that he and Lamont were good to go, parked, and walked up to Freeman. The red buds were just coming into bloom. Early this year.

Freeman's face turned hard. "What the hell do you want?"

"Just to talk. There're some things you need to know. All you've got to lose is about thirty minutes. If you don't listen, you could lose a lot more than that."

"Your help, shit." He spat and gestured down the road. "Buzz off."

"If you think Czerny's death will be the end of this, you're a fool." I nodded in the direction of the workmen listening to our conversation. "You want to discuss this in front of your crew?"

Freeman glared at me, looked at his crew, and then turned back to me. "Make it quick."

We headed to my car, got in, and took off down a county road. Past experience told me my cellphone didn't have service there. Maybe his wouldn't either. Mahaffey and Lamont needed time to hit Freeman's business office.

"An eyewitness says you killed Fannin," I told Freeman.

He flipped me off. "The hell you say."

"Don't bother. You did it, and Janak knows you did it. He ordered the hit."

"You don't know what you're talking about." His voice rose an octave.

"To Janak, you're just a loose end, one that can point to him. That's something he can't afford, especially now that things are starting to unravel. You're probably the first name on Janak's hit list."

"Bullshit." He looked down, squeezed his eyes shut, and then pinched the bridge of his nose.

"Have it your way, but I've got my sources in this town. Word is that Janak's given Sobota the go-ahead to take you out."

Freeman narrowed his eyes. Sweat beaded on his upper lip. "That can't be true. They wouldn't do that."

I chuckled. "After what Janak had you do to Fannin, you still think that?"

He squirmed.

I looked at him and back at the road. "Call it like you see it, but at least make sure your life insurance is paid up."

He slumped in his seat. "Why are you telling me this? If you think I killed Fannin, why do you care what happens to me?"

"You don't mean a damn to me, but you're my way to get to the big boys. If they take you out, there's no one left to nail them."

"What do you expect me to do? Go to the cops?"

I laughed. "Sobota?"

"No, the feds or something."

"How well did that work for Fannin? He was talking to the Rangers. And these boys have a mole in the FBI."

"FBI? Shit. Who then?"

"It's up to you. But think about whether you want to sit idly by while Sobota comes to kill you. I'd go after him first."

"Is that what you want me to do?"

"What I want's beside the point. For your own sake, you need to look at the facts."

Freeman dropped his head and shook it, his fists clenched in his lap. "Damn, everything was rocking along until about a week ago. Now it's a huge shit-storm. Just out of the blue. How did this happen?"

We pulled up back at his worksite. As he opened the door, I called out, "Did you enjoy Omaha? Pretty quick trip, wasn't it?"

His eyes flashed. He stared at me without saying a word, got out, and slammed the door.

Confirmation. He was the *pinche culero* who had attacked Kathy.

*　　*　　*　　*

Mahaffey and Lamont had a Ryder truck and were costumed in dark suits, ties, and starched white shirts. We had even ginned up fake badges and a fake warrant for them to flash.

Freeman had been diverted long enough. Mahaffey and Lamont had all the computers and paper files in the truck and were on the road out of town before Freeman got word and could get back to the office. They had found the secretary alone. Mahaffey laughed about her repeatedly calling Freeman, but to no avail.

We called Esquivel and told him the FBI had raided Freeman Construction and seized everything. It wouldn't take long for the word to spread. I felt a smile, whether or not it showed on my face. The conversation seemed over when Esquivel called out, "Hey, we needed to talk anyway. We're making the Janak machine hurt in ways we didn't predict."

"How so?"

"*Narcotraficantes*. With all the rumors, the drug dealers smell weakness, and they've cut the Janaks off from their piece of the action."

I grinned. "How can you not love watching *capullos* fight each other?"

Chapter 12: Turks and Caicos

We trailed Freeman and Samaniego. Within the week, Freeman took his kids out of school and sent them and his wife away. To cover the possibility that he might follow later, Mahaffey trailed his wife, who ended up at a house backing up to a bayou near Lake Jackson—a house belonging to her sister.

Freeman himself carried on in Komensky but didn't go after Sobota as I had hoped.

The same day Freeman's wife left, we saw Samaniego dragging bags from his house. Lamont followed him all the way to Houston Intercontinental, where Samaniego boarded a flight to Turks and Caicos.

After reporting what he had found trailing Samaniego, Lamont and I sat on the hotel patio. I enjoyed another Cohiba, but Lamont stared off into space. He tugged at his clothes and crossed and uncrossed his arms. Lately he had been doing more of that sort of thing. I failed to reflect on what bothered him. Stupid me.

*　　*　　*　　*

Someone had to bear the burden of checking on Samaniego in the Caribbean. Michelson, the owner of the agency, decided the problem needed his expertise.

Three days later, Michelson called me just as I had lit an Arturo Fuentes Churchill. Lavishly spreading money apparently accomplishes a lot in the Turks and Caicos. Michelson quickly learned Samaniego had made the hop to Providenciales, where Michelson offered twenty-dollar bills to tax drivers until he found one who knew of an American who had recently rented a cottage near Leeward Settlement.

That driver got a fare.

"Did you get a glimpse of Samaniego when you drove by?"

"No, but we met by my playing the Texas card."

"The Texas card?" I puffed my cigar.

"Yeah, a taxi driver dropped me and my six-pack of beer off down the road from the cottage. I poured part of a beer on my clothes and gave three of them to the taxi driver."

"Pretending to be drunk is the Texas card?"

"Nacho, dammit, this is *my* story. Let me tell it my way."

My laughing seemed to mollify Michelson, so he continued. "I staggered down the road toward the cottage loudly singing 'The Eyes of Texas.' "

"Samaniego's an Aggie."

Michelson chuckled. "Must be. He called me a *pinche* tea sip. The University of Texas/Texas A&M rivalry worked well for me. At his cottage, I wandered into the yard, collapsed against the front door, and kept singing. He pulled the door open, and I fell at his feet. It was Samaniego, all right."

"What did he do?"

"That's when he called me a *pinche* tea sip. Then he told me to get the hell off his property or he'd call the cops."

"Did he call them?"

"No, I grabbed his trouser legs and pulled myself up, spilling a little beer on him in the process. Verisimilitude, you know? And for the hell of it." Michelson chuckled.

"Sounds like you had fun on this trip."

"Had? I'm thinking of extending my stay. I met an interesting lady in the bar last night."

"I'll bet you did." I rolled my eyes. "You and Mahaffey."

After a pause, Michelson asked, "How do you want to get Samaniego's location to Janak?"

"Not another anonymous tip. Janak's no idiot. Sooner or later he'll figure out it's us stirring things up."

"My thought, too."

I tapped my cigar to drop the ash and pinched the bridge of my nose, eyes shut tight. *How could we out him without outing ourselves?* Writing his friends came to me. "How's the island's selection of postcards?"

"Hah. Good enough."

"One more thing. Do you think you can set up surveillance cameras on Samaniego's place without him knowing? That way we can see what happens when the Komensky boys come after him."

Michelson snorted. "Who the hell taught you to do *that* shit?"

We got the addresses of Samaniego's secretary and the number-two administrator at the college. Michelson sent them both forged postcards in Samaniego's name and included his return address. "Hope to hear from you soon," the postcards read.

*   *   *   *

Not much happened while we were diverted by Samaniego's lark in the Turks and Caicos. With the postcards in the mail, I called Esquivel. "What are you hearing on the street?"

"People are nervous, but just waiting for another shoe to drop, you know? Uh, hold on." He called out to someone but didn't cover the phone. "Hey, *vato, que tal?*"

Another voice came through, garbled.

"Sure thing, man. Got you covered, but look, I gotta take this call right now, okay?" It *must* have been okay, because Esquivel came back. "Where was I? Oh, yeah, people are just waiting to see what happens, you know?"

73

"It's up to us to make something happen."

"Yeah, what do you want me to do?"

I pursed my lips and thought for a moment. "Okay, pass around the word that, after the raid on his office, Freeman cut a deal with the feds. That he put the finger on Sobota for Mark Fannin's murder. And say that Bruhn is good with making Sobota the patsy."

"That'll piss Sobota off."

"That's the idea."

Chapter 13: The Numbers Dwindle

Tired of losing gin rummy games to Lamont, I spent a few days back in San Antonio catching up on paperwork. Done with that, getting ready for another stint in Komensky required a long session at the Laundromat savoring the odor of chlorine bleach, watching the dryer spin, and trying to read the graffitied wall. My cellphone broke the monotony. Mahaffey was minding the fort in Komensky, and his name showed on the screen. I glanced around and saw only one other person, a heavy-set woman across the room folding clothes.

"What's up?" I asked Mahaffey.

"Not up, but down. There's been another death."

I leaned forward and spoke softly. "Who? How?"

"Some old guy out baling hay found the mayor, Lewis Janak. He was lying in a field with a bullet through his forehead. The day before, our bug in Martin Janak's office caught Martin telling Lewis that the loss of the drug rake-off was too big to let go. He ordered Lewis to get the drug dealers to 'come to Jesus,' as he put it."

I snorted. "It seems Lewis was the one who went to Jesus."

"Or somewhere."

*   *   *   *

I returned to Komensky for Lewis Janak's funeral. He lay in an open casket, assuring me he had been nailed for sure. Throughout the service I resisted the urge to drive a wooden stake through his heart and wondered why Les Sobota wasn't there.

After the funeral, I sidled up to Esquivel. "Any idea where Sobota is?"

Esquivel's eyes turned from side to side, checking out the room. "We shouldn't be seen together." He took a deep breath. "Nobody's seen Sobota for a few days." He looked around again. "I'm out of here, *vato*."

*　　*　　*　　*

We found out where Sobota had been. Michelson sent me a Federal Express package with a copy of materials he had sent to the FBI and the Turks and Caicos authorities. The package included a thumb-drive with a video of Sobota entering Ruben Samaniego's cottage in the night and strangling him. The infrared camera left no doubt of the killer's identity. Mahaffey got us travel information proving Sobota had made a quick trip to Turks and Caicos.

I leaned back from watching the video and grinned. *One more down.* A Cohiba and some Maker's Mark served for another celebration. Mahaffey joined me. Lamont's chin trembled, and he slipped his hands in his pocket, his face blank. He left without saying a word.

We sent copies of the package to Martin Janak and to Sobota himself. That probably kept them up at night. It should have.

*　　*　　*　　*

Two more dominoes fell at the end of the week. I had just returned to my motel room from the breakfast bar, when Mahaffey banged on my door. Lamont and he stood outside.

"Grab a seat," Mahaffey said, and he turned on my TV.

I took the one chair, and Mahaffey sat on the edge of the bed. Lamont stood in the back corner of the room with crossed arms, a Gideon's Bible in his hands. Les Sobota peered out from the TV screen, standing in the same place where he had announced Czerny's death. American and Texan flags stood sentinel again. Voices from behind the cameras peppered him with questions. Sobota's eyes were glassy until he closed them, looked down, and rubbed his temples. Things were closing in on the son-of-a-bitch. Gratifying.

76

He looked up, took a deep breath, and waved a paper in front of him. "I'd like to read a statement, please. It will answer most of your questions." His voice was strained. The noise subsided, and Janak continued in a monotone: "About eight o'clock yesterday evening, Komensky County Deputy Sheriff Howard Bruhn and I attempted to serve an arrest warrant on Carl Freeman, a local contractor. We obtained the warrant based on evidence that Mr. Freeman was involved with Thomas Czerny in college district corruption. Because of a personal relationship with the suspect, I made an error of judgment . . ." Sobota paused and looked down before continuing, ". . . for which I take full responsibility."

A glint of light that could have been a tear formed in the inside corner of an eye. Academy Award material. He spoke again. "Instead of surrounding the house with a team and demanding that the suspect come out with his hands up, Deputy Bruhn and I just walked up to the front door and knocked. The suspect fired through the window, killing Deputy Bruhn. The suspect was then killed in a brief firefight." He paused again and shuffled his papers. "Bear in mind that this coincides with an apparent federal investigation of Mr. Freeman's business, and that Mr. Freeman recently sent his family away to live with relatives. We surmise that the investigation was more pressure than he could deal with."

It was hard to figure this one. Sobota had probably shot Freeman and used the occasion as an opportunity to get rid of Bruhn, too. But the account Sobota gave was possible. We would never know the truth. It was no occasion for grief either way.

Sobota paused, folded his prepared statement, and turned as if to leave. A tumult of questions poured forth. He looked down, and then leaned back to the microphone with a reddening face. "That's all I am prepared to say at this time. We'll not release details of our investigation, as it is now moot, and there's no point in further besmirching the reputations of these men who were friends to all of us and some of whose families still live among us."

"Goddamn," Mahaffey said. "These bastards play for keeps."

I waved my hand. "It's worked well for us so far."

Lamont slammed the Bible on the dresser. I turned to him. "Lamont, we've discussed this before. These are their own damned rules."

He pointed an index finger at me, his eyes cold. "And that makes it okay for us to play by them?"

"You're pretty casual about Freeman trying to kill my daughter. Once they did that, yeah, I'm okay playing by their rules. No tears from *me* for these bastards." He ran a hand through his hair and shook his head. "I didn't sign up to help your personal vendetta." His voice was loud and higher pitched than normal. "I'm done setting people up to be killed. What they've done doesn't excuse what we do. I'm heading back to San Antonio. If Michelson wants to fire me, so be it." He strode out of the room, slamming the door behind him.

Mahaffey tilted his head and lifted his eyebrows. "Cut him some slack. Lamont's been pretty upset. He told me he's been praying about this."

An image of my grandfather appeared in my mind—a drunken, embittered old man despised by those he had lived among. Was I on that path? I shook the idea out of my head. These *asquerosos* had to die.

Chapter 14: Culmination

Two nights later found me at Sammy's Night Club in Hallettsville. The jukebox played George Strait, smoke and stale beer filled the air, and flashing neon signs revealed rusty branding irons on the wall. With my back to the door, I stood at the bar, swallowed the last of my Dos Equis, and looked around for Esquivel.

"Bartender, another beer." He slid one to me, and I slid a five-spot back to him.

Esquivel had asked for this meeting. He feared Sobota had pegged him as the source of rumors and blamed me for approaching him at Lewis Janak's funeral. Esquivel was the closest thing to a friend I had in Komensky. If he needed help, I had to give it, but an hour had passed since we were to meet. The evening wore on, but one looked familiar.

The front door banged open, and Sheriff Sobota filled the doorway. "Hey, Detective Nacho!" he called out. "You a regular here? Or are you waiting on somebody?"

I took another gulp of beer and looked at him, keeping my expression flat.

"Let me guess who you're waiting for," he said. "It wouldn't be a punk-ass constable, would it? One that's been a little chummy with you?"

I swigged again and turned my back to him. He walked up to the bar and stood beside me. Others moved away. "Barkeep," he called out. "Gimme a Bud."

When he got his beer, he took a long swig and turned to face me. "Your boy Esquivel—he should have kept his nose out of things that weren't his business, you know?"

"What's it to me?"

"What's it to you is he's dead. And that's a state of affairs you should be giving some thought to."

My bowels knotted. *Esquivel, dead?* I willed myself not to give Sobota the satisfaction of a visible reaction. I turned and looked him up and down. "You know, there's been a lot of people who turned out to need life insurance—your deputy Bruhn, Thomas Czerny, Ruben Samaniego, Lewis Janak, and Benjamin Freeman. My guess is there's at least a couple more to fall. Say, maybe, Martin Janak and you."

I put my beer on the bar, stepped around Sobota, and headed out the door. He called out to my back. "Before he had his accident, you know, Esquivel was pretty talkative. He told us all about your gossip plan. I guess *chisme's* not going to work for you anymore."

I kept walking. Sobota followed me. "One more thing, pal. You heard from that black guy lately? Lamont Washington, was it?"

I turned to face him. "What about Lamont?"

"My condolences to his family."

Sobota turned and stepped back into the bar. I stood by my car and called Michelson at home. "Did Lamont make it back to the office?"

"No, why? Isn't he with you?"

"I thought he was with *you.* Long story. Sobota says Lamont's dead."

"Dead? What happened?"

Michelson listened to my account and then said, "I'll be there in a few hours."

"No, boss. Better you don't. Better that we didn't have this conversation. Let me take care of the—sheriff." I spat.

*   *   *   *

I knocked on Mahaffey's motel-room door. He let me in and motioned toward the chair. He pulled two cold Coronas out of an ice chest and handed one to me. I downed the whole thing and, elbows on knees, dropped my head into my hands.

Mahaffey studied me for a bit and took a sip. "That bad, huh?"

"Yeah. They got Lamont."

He dropped the hand with his beer to his side. "What do you mean?'"

"Sobota told me they killed him, and he never made it back to San Antonio."

"Goddamn." Mahaffey shook his head. "Well, they had to figure it was us behind all the rumors. We should've known they'd come after us."

I slammed my fist on the side table. "They were supposed to come after *me!* Stupid! I was blind to the risk they'd come after you or Lamont."

"Come on, Nacho. We're big boys. Neither of us took this job because we wanted a nanny."

"I shouldn't have let him go. I should have told him I was sorry."

Mahaffey shook his head. "But you *weren't* sorry, and he knew that. If anything, Lamont got careless. It could have been any of us. It just turned out to be him."

I waved my empty Corona bottle. "Give me another."

Mahaffey crossed his arms, looked at me, and bit his lower lip. "No, not a good idea. You'll thank me in the morning."

Shooting him the finger, I stomped out of the room and slammed the door behind me.

*   *   *   *

The next morning, my head felt better than if Mahaffey had given me more beer. He manned our listening station while I sat outside the Komensky County Courthouse, trying to put Lamont out of my mind.

When Martin Janak came to work, I gave him a few minutes and followed him to his office, breezing past his secretary's objections like before. He leapt to his feet and gestured at me with a sword-shaped letter-opener. "Look here, Perez, you can't keep barging in here. Get out before I call the sheriff."

I raised my hands, palms out. "Sobota's who we need to talk about. You've had time to look at the package we sent you?"

"Nothing to do with me. What the sheriff does on vacation is his affair."

A laugh erupted from my throat. "You don't really think a judge and jury will buy that? You've been to too many rodeos."

He stared at me wide-eyed for a moment, collapsed in his chair, and dropped his chin to his chest. He pinched the bridge of his nose and looked up. "You son-of-a-bitch. You've destroyed everything."

"If you hadn't had Mark Fannin killed, you might have gotten away with a couple of people at the college taking the fall. His lawyer wouldn't have paid me to go farther than that."

Janak blew air out between his teeth and waved dismissively.

I leaned forward, my hands on his desk. "What's your FBI mole telling you about this?"

He sat upright and his eyes narrowed. "Up yours."

I held my hands up and fluttered my fingers. "Little birdies are all around."

He shook his head. "So what do you want?"

I stood up straight and stared into his eyes. "You need to think hard about what's best for you."

He leaned forward. "What do you mean?"

Helping myself to a chair, I continued. "With the Caribbean video, the financial evidence from the college, and the other evidence we've accumulated, your whole machine's coming down. Not you, not Sobota, not anybody can stop it. Think about the least bad way for you to come out of this."

Janak tilted his chair back and played with his letter opener. "You must have something to share, or you wouldn't be here."

I cleared my throat. "It's probably true that you haven't personally killed anybody. You just ordered others to do it, and the only one of those left is Sobota. So which of you is going down harder, and what can you do to see that it's not you?"

He gestured with the letter-opener as if it were a real sword. "So you recommend turning rat?"

I leaned forward and handed him a note. "That's the name and phone number of the FBI agent-in-charge in San Antonio. Call him and spin things your way. Say you never intended for people to get hurt. At first you believed the accident stories Sobota was peddling, and then you were afraid of him. He was totally off the reservation."

Janak sat silently, looking down at the note. He folded it in half and then in half again. Then he spread it out on the desk.

"It's up to you," I said.

Janak remained silent for a while longer and looked up. "I'll give it some thought."

"You do that."

*   *   *   *

I headed back to the monitoring station in the former dentist's office. By the time I got there, Mahaffey had extracted an audio file of my conversation with Janak. We emailed it to every radio station within a radius of a hundred miles.

At first, the stations ignored it, but then KTXM, a country station out of Hallettsville, ran it on the air. KTXM billed itself as Texas Thunder Radio, and the thunder from that broadcast resonated throughout a wide swath. Another station ran the file, and then another and another. Within a week, radio played it throughout the state. Even television stations played the audio clip while showing a photograph of Martin Janak.

The file's wide dissemination seemed likely to prompt an encounter between Janak and Sobota. Not wanting to miss it, Mahaffey and I traded off trailing Janak. Mornings were my shift; his, the afternoons.

The final death knell for the Komensky machine rang when the Texas Attorney General announced a probe. The evidence was too blatant for Janak to buy his way out. My Maker's Mark and my Perdomo Habano cigar were especially good that night.

The morning after the announcement, I picked up Janak's trail and followed him to the courthouse. His office looked out over the main entrance, but his reserved parking space was in the rear, a few yards from a back door. He pulled into his space and exited the car. As he did so, he slipped his hand into the side pocket of his coat. I thought nothing of it, and he headed into the courthouse.

I parked in the shade of a large pecan tree, rolled down the windows, and broke out a Styrofoam cup of coffee. The coffee kept me occupied until a loud pop came from the courthouse. Looking around revealed no obvious source. Then Mahaffey called.

"Nacho. I'm on the bug. Somebody shot a gun in Janak's office."

I hopped out of my car, sprinted for the back entrance, and took the stairs two at a time. Janak's secretary wept at the entrance to his office. A sheriff's deputy inspected a body with a bloody head flopped on Janak's desk.

The secretary pulled the tissues from her eyes. "It's you. You made him do this. He was always good to me."

I caught a glimpse of the body's face. Janak, the King of Komensky, sat slumped, head in a pool of blood with a 9mm Ruger in his hand. A real suicide in Komensky. Who knew real suicides actually happened in Komensky?

The deputy looked up and pointed at me. "Sir, you're going to have to leave. We can't have the public tromping through here."

"Certainly, officer, on my way." I headed out of his office past Janak's secretary.

She wiped her tears again. "Why? Why did you come here and turn over our lives like cans of garbage?"

I glanced in the direction of Janak and glared at her. "Haven't you thought about the lives wrecked by these people? What about the families of Mark Fannin, Tommy Araya, Florencio Narvaez, Jorge Esquivel, my friend Lamont Washington, and my daughter's fiancé Benjamin McGinty? What about the near-death of my daughter and her infant son?" I stopped and closed my eyes, willing myself to stop shaking. "Just think of *me* as the garbage man."

*   *   *   *

Only Sheriff Sobota remained. Straight-out shooting a law enforcement officer still seemed a bad idea. Around noon, my thoughts went to food. Maybe an idea would come to me over lunch.

I hadn't been back to Tommy's Tacos since his wife Mercedes confronted me. Today seemed a good time to look for a different response. The same blue tarp covered part of the roof, and no cop cars were in the customer lot. Still, Sobota might come. I parked in the rear, next to the dumpster where my car couldn't be seen from the street.

Sobota wasn't inside, so I took a seat facing the front, close to the kitchen.

The waitress's eyes passed over me and turned back. She stared, stepped to the register, and whispered to Mercedes Araya, pointing at me. Mercedes' eyes followed the waitress's pointed finger. She nodded to the waitress and gave change to the customer at the register. When the customer headed for the door, she approached me.

"You're back," she said in a flat tone.

I nodded. "A lot's happened since the last time."

She returned my nod. "It has." A tear formed next to her nose. "It hasn't brought Tommy back." She leaned her head forward, squeezed her eyes shut, and pinched the bridge of her nose. After a few deep breaths, she looked up. "Tommy would have been glad to see the machine break up. At least you did that." She took more deep breaths.

A waitress passed by, and Mercedes said, "Take his order."

The *carne guisada* had been so good before it seemed a good bet again. My eyes lingered on a Dos Equis at the next table, but iced tea seemed more prudent until Sobota was out of circulation. The *carne guisada* was great, and the homemade flour tortillas were even better. I was mopping up the last of the sauce with a tortilla when steps sounded behind me. Silence descended on the room.

Not good, dammit. Not good at all. Hands palm-down on the table, I pushed myself up and, as nonchalantly as possible, turned to face the kitchen, which put my back to most of the restaurant.

"Les Sobota, the man of the hour."

The mostly empty whiskey bottle in his left hand explained his flushed face and the odor hanging about him. The pistol in his right hand, held at his hip, explained his purpose. He tossed away the bottle. "Nobody likes a smartass, Nacho." He spat on the floor and slurred his speech.

Behind me, chairs scraped on the floor, and footsteps moved away from us.

"You feeling real satisfied with yourself, right now? Well, don't." He gestured toward me with the pistol.

I waved my hand around the room. "You're not going to shoot me in front of all these people." More scraping chairs and more footsteps.

"You stupid sonuvabitch." He spread his arm wide and high, almost losing his balance. "You've fixed it so I've got nothing to lose. The best I can do is take you now, before they come for me." From the noise, the entire restaurant was trying to evacuate.

He had a point. My Government Model .45 sat holstered inside my rear waistband, under my guayabera, seven rounds in the magazine plus one in the chamber. Sobota had what looked like a full-sized Glock in his hand, probably a 9mm. So, he probably had twice my rounds, maybe more. But running out of ammo wasn't my big worry. He would shoot me before my gun got out of the holster.

I slumped, stepped back a couple of steps, pulled over the chair I had been sitting in, and leaned on its backrest. "Man, you caught me at a bad time. My gout's killing me."

Sobota's eye's widened, and he raised his left hand. "You think I give a—"

I slung the chair at Sobota's head. He hadn't been distracted much. A round zipped past my ear as I lunged to the right. Chaos enveloped the room as the remaining customers and staff screamed, scrambled, and dove to the floor. My feint had let me get my gun out, but before I could level on Sobota, one of his rounds slammed into my abdomen. *Damn.* My round went wide, but it scared Sobota enough that his next round did, too.

Pain stabbed in my belly, but I pushed it out of my mind. *Sight picture, dammit. Sight picture.* I tried for Sobota's center of mass with another round but couldn't hold myself together. My round went low. Sobota staggered and dropped to his knees, and a red splotch spread across his right thigh, just as another round slammed into my chest. I staggered, and my vision started to narrow. I clenched my teeth and tried to focus but couldn't hold my arms up. My gun sagged, and darkness closed in. Just before everything went black, an enormous blast filled the room.

Chapter 15: And Then There Were None

Beep. Beep. Beep.

Everything seemed fuzzy except the beeping. *What's making that noise?*

"Daddy? Daddy? This is Kathy. Can you hear me?"

I turned my head, my eyes fluttering. The light and pain from the movement made me snap them back shut.

"He moved his head. Daddy, it's me." A hand grasped mine, and I grasped back.

"He's responding. Nurse, come quickly. He's responding."

Another person took my hand. "Squeeze my hand, please," she said.

I pressed.

"That's good," she said. "Can you show me two fingers?" I tried, but don't know if any fingers came up.

"He's better," Kathy's voice said.

A sigh, and another voice. "I suppose. Look, when he came in, I wouldn't have bet a cup of coffee on his chances. So, yeah, maybe better, but still in the woods."

Someone adjusted my covers, and I faded out.

*   *   *   *

The beeping came back. I blinked, trying to keep my eyes open. The room around me came into focus. Cool fluorescent light revealed monitoring equipment and a stand holding drip-bags beside my bed. A curtain hung from a track affixed to the acoustic tile ceiling. Tubes stuck up my nose, and others snaked down from the drip-bags to needles piercing my arms.

A hospital room. What happened? Fog clouded my mind. Someone hovered over me.

"Mr. Perez, can you hear me? On a scale of one to ten, how bad is your pain?"

Too much to focus on. Whatever mumbles came out weren't likely intelligible.

A woman held a bright light to my eyes, which instinctively scrunched shut. "Please try to keep your eyes open." Fingers held my eyelids apart. The light stabbed my eyes, and I inhaled sharply.

When the light went away, I held my eyes shut and took deep breaths, which brought piercing spasms to my chest. A voice said, "Good. Your pupils look good, Mr. Perez."

I faded out again.

*　　*　　*　　*

More beeping. I opened my eyes and fought to keep them that way. The beeping sped up. A female face appeared above mine. A stethoscope drooped from her neck, and she wore a scrub top. *A nurse.*

"Mr. Perez, welcome back. How are you feeling?"

My parched mouth and throat made it difficult to talk. "Thirsty," I croaked.

The nurse offered ice-chips on a spoon. Never had simple water seemed so good.

"Where am I? What happened?"

"You're in San Antonio Military Medical Center. They airlifted you in from Komensky. You were in pretty rough shape."

My mind raced to take that in. A small piece clicked into place. "Sobota, the crooked son-of-a-bitch."

"That sums up the gossip around here," she said as she pulled the stand holding my drip bags closer. "Let's try again on your pain. On a scale of one to ten, how bad is it?"

"I don't know. Keeping still, it's not too bad."

"Sorry. We've got to get you moving. Pneumonia and blood clots are bad things." She pulled the covers down to my waist and then raised the bed. I leaned forward and gasped. Phantoms shoved swords through me, and I quickly fell back the few inches I had risen.

"That was a nine or a ten."

"OK," she said. "We'll try again in a little while."

"More ice, please."

Ice in my mouth was my last memory before fading out yet another time.

*　　　*　　　*　　　*

Someone shook my shoulder. I blinked my eyes open and found the nurse leaning over me. "Mr. Perez, we need to try again getting you up." She cranked the bed as far as it would go and pulled me up. I whimpered, despite my resolve not to.

"If you want to get out of here, tough guy, we've got to get you on your feet."

I gasped, but that only added to the hurt. "Is your name Ratched?"

She snorted. "You just hope I'm not any worse than *she* was." She paused, and then persisted. "We've got to get you up and moving, and, you know, your daughter's downstairs. Let's get you up before she comes back. She's been by your side a long time."

91

I gritted my teeth and squeezed my eyes shut as the nurse swung my legs over the side of the bed. I sat, breathing deeply, building resolve to stand. The deep breaths were necessary, but the piercing they caused in my chest added to the underlying ache there and in my abdomen.

"That's enough feeling sorry for yourself. Feet on the deck." She grinned. "Your daughter told me you were a Marine DI. I'm going to have you doing laps in the corridor."

I scooted toward the edge of the bed and eased weight onto my feet, moving to a standing position.

"Good," she said. "Now come forward."

I shuffled three or four steps.

"More," she said. "Give me more."

When I got across the room, she raised the tubes from my drip-bags, which kept them from tangling, and had me turn around. "Now, march back to the bed."

One step, and Kathy walked in, carrying a covered Styrofoam cup. "Daddy, it's just like you to finally wake up and start walking when I go for coffee."

My hand reached out for her involuntarily, but I winced and dropped it to my side. She set down the coffee and rushed to my side, helping me to move back toward the bed. When there, I collapsed into a sitting position. Several minutes elapsed before I let her swing my legs up to lay me flat.

"I'm so happy to see you up, Daddy. If it hadn't been for that woman with the shotgun, I—" She choked up.

Woman with the shotgun? I couldn't pull that up from my memory, such as it was. Everything since facing off against Sobota was hazy.

"He's had enough for now," the nurse said. She adjusted the roller clamp on the IV tubing, and again I faded out—something I had been doing a lot of.

*   *   *   *

The next day, we walked more. The nurse lured me with the promise of real food. To my dismay, Jell-O counted as real food.

Most of what happened came back to me, and I explained it to Kathy. But the shotgun eluded me. "What's this about a woman with a shotgun?"

"Mercedes Araya. She pulled a shotgun from behind her counter and let the sheriff have both barrels. She saved your life."

"How did you hear that?"

"She came to check on you. We had a nice talk." Kathy smiled, and her eyes twinkled. "She's a nice-looking lady, about your age."

I shook my head. "She blames me for her husband's death. With some reason."

*   *   *   *

Michelson called to let me know that Lamont Washington's memorial service was the next day. They had never found his body. That made me walk more. I had to be in shape to go. I would be.

*   *   *   *

Kathy got me to the East Side Church early enough to snag a parking place across Center Street. She carried Bennie, who now had pudgy cheeks. Angel Marrero, another Michelson and Associates operative, wheeled my chair up the ramp to a sixties-era wing tacked to the back of a much older musty-smelling masonry sanctuary with a soaring ceiling and narrow stained-glass windows. Angel set me in a wheelchair space at the back, and we watched others trickle in.

Michelson and Mahaffey both came, shook my hand, and sat in the row in front of me. Michelson turned and leaned back. "Wasn't sure you'd make it. How you doing?"

I raised my hands palms up. "Pretty good, considering the two extra holes."

He twitched his cheek and grinned. "Damn, Nacho. You got through twenty years in the Corps without getting shot. You losing your touch?"

Kathy put her finger to her lips. "Shhh." The trickle of incoming guests had grown, and an organist played "Will the Circle Be Unbroken."

The service was about to begin when two young men helped a stooped older woman to the front row. Her hat towered above her head, and tears glistened on her cheeks. *Lamont's mother.* He had introduced me to her when I once dropped him off at her house. She took her seat just before the preacher read scripture.

Midway into the service, Lamont's brother Kordell climbed to deliver the eulogy. He pulled a sheet of paper from his coat pocket and surveyed the room, eyes momentarily pausing on me. He talked of Lamont's and his childhood together, of Lamont's hopes and dreams, of Lamont's affection for his nieces and nephews, and of the love and respect he gave their mother.

Kordell tilted his head up, closed his eyes and took a deep breath. Looking back at the assembly, he spoke of Lamont's deep religious faith and his commitment to righteousness. Kordell paused and looked at me again. "Lamont was committed to doing right even when it cost him, even when it meant refusing to do what his employer wanted. We should all try to have as much moral courage as Lamont. When faced with a difficult choice, we should ask what Lamont would have done."

Kordell continued looking at me for a moment. Then he descended from the pulpit and returned to sit beside his mother.

After the service, the casket was wheeled out to an organ rendition of "Soon and Very Soon." Kathy gathered Bennie, and Angel moved behind my chair, waiting for the sanctuary to clear. The family followed the casket, and Lamont's mother turned to me as she came down the aisle. When she got to the rear, she stopped and pointed. The strength of the frail woman's voice surprised me.

"You, Nacho Perez. You got my boy killed." The organ stopped, and silence fell over the room.

I winced and nodded my head. "I can't tell you how sorry I am. Lamont was a good man."

She took a deep breath and straightened up from her stoop. "You'll get over being sorry, but he's not getting over being dead."

My eyes moistened, and my head dropped. I hoped for the mercy the preacher had spoken of.

Kathy grabbed my shoulder with her free arm. "You got the truth, Daddy."

"The truth." Lamont's mother spat the words. "Your truth got Lamont dead. And that Mr. Fannin and all the others Lamont told me about. How many others? When you stacked up all the bodies, did you count how many your truth made dead?"

My chest heaved with sobs.

An image of my grandfather appeared, pointing his finger at me and laughing.

Excerpt from In Search of El Dorado

Another Nacho Perez story

I drove out of the ranch compound and headed back down the winding ranch road to the highway. My A/C labored in the heat, and road dust infiltrated the car. Fifteen minutes into the trip, I rounded a hill and came to a cattle trailer blocking the way. One side was jacked up, and a wheel lay on the ground. I stopped well short of the trailer and walked up to investigate.

As I drew near, four men, two on each side, came around from behind the trailer. All of them had ax handles. My .45 was in the glove box. My getting to the car before they got me wasn't likely, but you go with what you've got. I made a break and tried to sprint to the car. Moments later, an axe handle knocked my feet out from under me. Pain erupted in my shoulder. I curled into a fetal position with my arms around my head as blows from ax handles and boots rained on me. It was all an agonizing blur until I passed out.

Mother of God, it hurts. What happened? Where am I? I wriggled my limbs. It was excruciating, but everything except my left arm seemed to work. I dozed. Pain again. There was only a faint glow of light in the sky. *It's evening now. I've lost most of the day.* I lay in a daze, and my entire body throbbed in agony. My tongue was swollen. *Water. God, I need water.*

I've got to get up. I rolled to try to get to my right hand and knees. I gasped. *Like a knife in my sides. Damn, broken ribs.* I caught my breath, braced myself, and tried to rise again. *Lord have mercy.*

I was on my knees, leaning on one hand. My left arm hung limply, my entire body screamed, and I fought the impulse to retch. I stayed in that position until I got the pain under control and then pulled one knee forward. The small additional weight on my right shoulder nearly made me collapse on my face. I paused again to get control. I heard a rustling in the brush and turned my head. *Armadillo.*

97

Lifting myself to a kneeling position was the hardest thing I've ever done. Pain surged through me, and I nearly fell, but I willed myself to stay erect. I fought again to control my breathing. I stayed in that position until the pain in my knees was worse than the pain throughout the rest of my body.

The sun hung low above the horizon, but it was noticeably higher than before. *Not evening. It's morning. I've lost a whole day and a night.* I already felt the sun's heat. *Worse is coming.* All I could see around me were scattered mesquites and prickly pear with occasional juniper. *God help me, I've got to get up.*

I braced myself and rose to my feet. The experience was horrific, and I was dizzy, but I stayed up. Again, I gagged, nearly vomiting.

Even from my feet, all I could see was thin brush and parched ground. No building, no power line, no pipeline, nothing. I staggered to a mesquite and grasped a branch for support. The sun was getting higher and hotter.

Water. I felt in the watch pocket of my Levis. The bastards at least left me my pen knife. *Thank God the blade's got a knob so I can open it with one hand.* A clump of prickly pear was just a few feet away. *Nopal, praise the Lord.* I trimmed at the thorns from a pad. With just one hand, the effort was clumsy and not entirely effective. Even so, I chewed it for the moisture. *Damn. I missed some of the little thorns.* It was disgusting stuff anyway. I'd never been a fan of nopalitos.

I staggered down barely visible vehicle tracks. The earth swayed under and around me. Mesquites appeared as apparitions, but I somehow kept on my feet and on the path of the vehicle that had brought me to this Godforsaken place.

As the sun neared its zenith, I took shelter under the spare shade of another mesquite, chewed more nopal, and tried not to think about pain. Or thorns. Or food. Or the flies buzzing in my face and ears. *Valle de la Sombra. Valley of the Shadow. Where the hell's some shade?*

Agony was constant and fatiguing, and I wanted nothing as much as I wanted to lie down, to give up. *If I do, I'll die.*

The sun moved on, and I did, too. The heat was suffocating. My exposed flesh blistered. Onward, one foot in front of the other. I paused for nopal. And onward again. I couldn't even find a stick to help me walk.

I kept staggering down the tracks, hoping to find something. To my right, I heard a sound like someone slightly turning the valve of a full scuba tank. *Cascabel.* A long, fat diamondback lay ahead and to the side. *At least something prospers out here.* I veered away from it.

When darkness approached, I found a sandy spot and descended as gingerly as I could. Pain kept me awake most of the night, but I must have drifted off sometime. Birds woke me at dawn.

Getting up was not as bad as the day before, but it's nothing I care to relive. I cut at nopal and not only chewed but swallowed. Then I resumed my trek.

I found a north-south gravel road. I turned right. *I was north of the highway when they waylaid me.* Half an hour later, I came to a dead end at a pumpjack. It was pumping. *Praise the Lord. People still come here.*

I turned around and headed back. Flies clustered around my eyes and mouth and in my popped sunburn blisters. During the morning, I passed at least two more pumpjacks. Just before noon, I heard the sound of an engine. I staggered on and heard voices. I croaked for help, but the volume of my voice was pitiful, and there was no sign they heard. Moments later, I saw men up a side road working on another pumpjack. I collapsed on the spot.

-o0o-

This excerpt is from "In Search of El Dorado," a short story included in the collection, *Nacho Perez, Private Eye.* If you would like to read more, please look for it on my Amazon Author Page:

http://tinyurl.com/k5jp3lz

Author Information

Kenneth Bennight is a husband, father, lawyer, former Marine, and native Texan who lives in San Antonio, Texas. And he's the grandfather of the cutest little boy on the face of the earth.

In addition to *The Truth Shall Make You Dead*, Kenneth is also the author of a collection of four Nacho Perez short stories called *Nacho Perez, Private Eye*.

Kenneth additionally has two Kindle-formatted, standalone short stories for sale on Amazon.

"Wild Man of the Navidad" is based on legends of a man-like creature in the bottom lands along Texas's Navidad River.

"Unlawful Combatants" considers how to deal with unconventional combatants outside today's political divide. An 1850s Comanche war party passes through a time warp to the present day. Having caught the Comanches raiding, the State of Texas sentences them to death. The case goes to the U.S. Supreme Court on whether the Comanches are prisoners of war instead of criminals.

He is also the author of Texas Law of Streets and Alleys: A Handbook. It is a legal handbook of interest to lawyers and real estate professionals who may from time to time confront issues such as who owns the streets, what private uses are consistent with public street rights, and what uses may the governing body not permit.

His Amazon Author Page is located at:

http://tinyurl.com/k5jp3lz

www.ingramcontent.com/pod-product-compliance
Lightning Source LLC
Chambersburg PA
CBHW020618130626
46552CB00003B/1022

* 9 7 8 1 9 4 6 4 1 8 0 0 5 *